DEATH IN THE ROUND

D1077892

Books you will enjoy
from Keyhole Crime:

DEATH IN THE ROUND

Anne Morice

KEYHOLE CRIME
London · Sydney

First published in Great Britain 1980 by
Macmillan London Limited

Copyright © Anne Morice 1980

Australian copyright 1982

This edition published 1982 by
Keyhole Crime, 15-16 Brook's Mews,
London W1A 1DR

ISBN 0 263 73808 6

Made and printed in Great Britain by
Cox & Wyman Ltd., Reading

ONE

'Ever been to Dearehaven?' I asked Robin during one of our leisurely Sunday breakfasts.

Being a Detective Inspector of the C.I.D., he feels more at home asking such questions than answering them and did not commit himself.

'It's in Dorset, isn't it?'

'That's right. Eighteen miles south-west of Dorchester. I got that from *The Good Food Guide*.'

'Wouldn't an atlas have served the purpose better?'

'No, because if I'm going to do three months there in rep. one of the first things you and Toby will want to know is whether there's a decent restaurant.'

'Oh, so that's what you'll be doing, is it?'

'I may. My agent is in favour of the idea.'

'When would you go?'

'20th May, starting with five weeks' rehearsal, which is far from bad. Dearehaven is on the coast too, so that wouldn't be bad either.'

'What plays are they doing?'

'Only one, so far as I'm concerned, and that's the least bad part of all. It's the new James Crowther. I haven't read it yet, but my agent says it's absolutely certain to come in. No guarantee that I'd come in with it, of course, but one has to take these gambles.'

'I find I understand less about the theatre every day,' Robin complained. 'Why should a new play by James Crowther, which is a name that even I recognise, get its try-out at an obscure place like Dearehaven?'

'Not all that obscure. In fact, it's become quite celebrated during the past few years.'

'But not on the regular pre-London circuit, surely?'

'It is for Jamie Crowther. Practically all his plays get their first airing at Dearehaven. He lives there, for a start, which makes it all nice and cosy, but I think the main reason is that the old legend in her time, Elfrieda Henshaw, has got him in her pocket.'

'Elfrieda Who?'

'Henshaw. Don't tell me you haven't heard of her famous Rotunda Theatre?'

'Not a word. What's so special about it?'

'It makes a profit, for one thing, which is about as special as you can get. And all due, so they say, to the inexhaustible tenacity and dedication of Elfrieda. She's in her mid-seventies now, but no sign of these fires burning low, I gather.'

'Why did she choose Dearehaven to blaze in?'

'She didn't choose it, it was thrust upon her. She's lived there all her life, the last of a long line of highly respectable, bloodsucking mill-owners or something. It was always mills that people of that sort owned, wasn't it?'

'Perhaps not in Dorset?'

'No, you're right; more likely breweries or cider. But the point is that they were the real old-fashioned, chapel-going, clogs-to-riches sort. Elfrieda was the only child and she never married. A very ugly duckling, by all accounts, and too clever for her own good. On the other hand, her father had such barrels of money that she must

6

have had a few offers. I suppose the truth is that she never found a suitor who was willing to devote his whole life to the theatre.'

'Oh, so this is not a new hobby?'

'No, a lifelong passion, but naturally her parents vetoed any sort of career in that line, they even regarded it as somewhat depraved to be a member of the audience. The most she was allowed to do was to organise tableaux for charity, which is where she doubtless got bitten by the impresario bug, and she seems to have spent every spare moment reading everything connected with the theatre that she could lay her hands on.'

Robin, whose attitude to the profession stops short of idolatry, remarked sadly:

'What a terribly dreary life! Is she a bit cracked?'

'As a coot, I should imagine; and pity there aren't more like her. However, the story has a happy ending. The old man left her everything, right down to the last stick and stone and, by a lucky chance, some of them were in a broken-down old building on the seafront, known as the Rotunda.'

'You mean to say the old hypocrite actually owned a theatre?'

'No, it wasn't one in his day. It housed what they grandly called the Maritime Museum, but it was pretty crummy, by all accounts and practically the only people who paid to go in were the board and lodging brigade, who had to find somewhere to get out of the rain. So eventually it was closed and left to rot. Then, just as it was about to be pulled down, to make way for a block of holiday flats, it fell into Elfrieda's lap. She's obviously a woman of vision and she immediately saw the possibilities of turning it into a theatre in the round, which was practically unknown in those days. Furthermore, she wanted all the most

7

talented actors and directors to come and work there, which in no time at all is what they were doing.'

'What was her secret?'

'It has great prestige nowadays, of course, but I gather that to start with it was done by a mixture of bully and bribe.'

'Oh, I see! So all this lovely money comes out of her own pocket? Nothing to do with audiences actually paying to get in?'

'Oh yes, they do that too, but you can't make a profit out of a provincial theatre of that size, even if you play to capacity at every performance. They all need subsidies of some kind and the rumour is that Elfrieda now gets more than she knows what to do with. Such is the present glory of the Rotunda that everyone, from the local rate-payers to the television companies, tumble over themselves to chip in.'

'So you won't be busking on Dearehaven pier to raise your fare back to London, even if the play flops?'

'I don't think there is a pier. It's much too genteel for that sort of thing.'

'Is there a decent restaurant, though?'

'Oh, you bet. They list three, but the Green Man sounds the most promising. Near the harbour and owned and managed by Mr and Mrs Banks. Mister does the cooking and he's noted for his specialities with lobster and crab. They have a few rooms too, so I might stay there when I go down next week for my interview.'

'You mean you have to go slogging all the way to Dorset to be interviewed? I thought you'd left that rung of the ladder behind you?'

'Yes, in theory, but Dearehaven is unique. I can't see Elfrieda putting herself out to come to London just to suit my convenience; nor can I believe that anyone sets foot on the Rotunda stage without her personal approval.

8

Besides, I'll need to look around and get fixed up in advance with somewhere to live which is at least technically within my means. I shouldn't imagine that a place which is renowned for its lobster and crab would be exactly cheap, would you?'

TWO

All rail journeys to Dearehaven are divided into three unequal parts. They begin with the long haul to Dorchester, followed by a wait of at least forty minutes, and ending with the slow, meandering trundle along the branch line to the coast. The last part is made even more uncomfortable by every seat being so positioned that the passenger has to sit with his back to the engine. This is not my favourite way of viewing the countryside, but I was sustained through my first experience of it by the reflection that what goes back must come forward and that, in the nature of things, we should all be facing the right way round on the return journey. However, this proved not to be the case and I was driven to the conclusion that the inhabitants of that part of Dorset, who differ from the rest of mankind in a number of ways, actually prefer to travel backwards and that British Rail are therefore compelled to go to a vast amount of time and trouble to shunt things around at each terminal, which could presumably also account for the forty minute wait.

However, I was shielded from all this on my first visit because on that occasion Len Johnson came to meet me at Dorchester Station and drove me the remaining eighteen miles in his Mini Clubman car.

Although this was our first meeting, I had heard something of Len, who turned out to be a rather nervous and self-conscious young man, with untidy brown hair and a bony, hungry-looking face, which flushed very easily, sometimes bringing tears to his eyes. He also had a somewhat abrasive manner, not rude or offhand, but a shade too head tossing and defensive for comfort. Another immediately noticeable thing about him was his accent, which fell somewhere between cockney and north country, but with overtones of pure King's Road. I guessed that he had started out with one, adopted another and had not yet got the mixture right.

This was his first season at Dearehaven, where he had been taken on at the express request of the Rotunda's leading light, James Crowther, who had seen some of his work in experimental theatres outside London. It was an unusual background for a director of the kind of lightweight, conventional comedies which Jamie wrote, but apparently Elfrieda had been equally enthusiastic. He had been engaged for the whole season and would also direct two other plays in the repertory.

The regular season ran from 5th April until the end of October, the programme changing each month, with one production being dropped to make way for a new one. Early in November rehearsals started for the Christmas pantomime, which ran for six weeks, and there then followed a fallow period in which the theatre was closed for re-decoration and plans laid for the spring and summer.

Much of this I had either known already or could have guessed, but it did not occur to me to point this out because no one likes to be interrupted while eulogising the object of his loyalty and devotion, and it had soon become abundantly clear that Len had been infected by Elfrieda's single-minded dedication to the Rotunda. In fact, the main impression I gained was that joining this company would

11

be more like entering a religious order than spending a few months in provincial rep.

On the other hand, this devotion to the cause had already brought me one bonus because, when the moment did come for me to speak and I started to thank him for coming all the way to meet me, he made it clear that it was not my convenience which had motivated him. He explained that he had intended, anyway, to drive over to Dorchester that morning, to look at a secondhand car which Elfrieda had seen advertised in the *Dearehaven Mercury*.

'Looks like a dud, though,' he added in grave tones, more appropriate to breaking the news that Big Ben had developed a crack down the middle and was in danger of falling over backwards.

He did not explain why an elderly woman of means should interest herself in dubious secondhand cars and it was not for me to enquire, so instead I asked him a few questions about the rest of the cast and the designer.

'Kyril Jones,' he said in reply to the last one, 'and he's another reason why I wanted to come to Dorchester this morning. He's got his eye on some bits and pieces in an old junk shop he thinks might do for the set and he asked me to take a look at them. You know him, do you?'

'Oh yes, awfully nice man. His mother was a Russian countess or something.'

'Oh, was she? And, in your view, is that what makes him awfully nice?'

'Goodness, no; although it does set him apart, I think, in his own view, anyway. I admire his work tremendously, but he has such a mumbly way of talking that I often find myself losing the thread.'

'He has no trouble making himself understood when he needs to,' Len said.

'Oh, sure! And very successful too, isn't he? It's rather surprising, in a way . . .'

'That he should be working in a back of beyond place like this, you were going to say?'

'Not at all. I was only thinking that most designers are so awfully definite about what they want and what they don't. It just came as a surprise that he should need advice about furniture.'

'He doesn't need it, but that's the way we do things here. We work as a team, not as individuals each doing our separate thing. And nobody pulls any rank either. As you'll find out.'

The last words sounded almost like a threat and, puzzled as well as deflated, I remained silent.

'Where shall I drop you?' he asked, as we reached the crest of a hill a few miles outside Dearehaven and caught a glimpse of the sparkling bay in the distance.

'I've booked a room at the Green Man. As it's only for one night,' I hastened to explain, realising that he had already managed to put me on the defensive. This time, however, his response was the exact opposite of what I had expected.

'Clever thinking!'

'It's as good as they say, is it?'

'Oh, I wouldn't know about that. Not in my class, I'm afraid, and I tend to become slightly revolted by the sight of a lot of rich people guzzling themselves stupid and then arguing with the waiter about the bill.'

I was trying to remember the last time I had heard someone arguing with a waiter about anything at all, when he added:

'More to the point, it's only five minutes' walk from the theatre. Which reminds me: Elfrieda would like to see you for a preliminary chat around twelve, if you can make it. After which, you'll get a chance to meet the rest of them at lunch.'

'The whole company?'

'Plus one extra. Don't look so worried, it's desperately informal. Elfrieda provides what she rather charmingly calls a cold collation in her office on working days. There's absolutely no rule about it, but everyone's welcome and they mostly turn up.'

'On the stage?'

'No, in her office. And an office like no other, I might add.'

'It must be, if it can accommodate that number. And who's the mysterious extra?'

'An eighteen-year-old retired juvenile delinquent, named Melanie.'

'Rather young for retirement?'

'Perhaps I should say reformed. That remains to be seen, but she is certainly managing to keep out of trouble at present.'

'How does she come to be mixed up with the Rotunda?'

'Mixed up hardly describes it. Elfrieda has adopted her.'

'Really? Whatever for?'

'Not legally, I should add. She's past the age for that, but she's out on probation and Elfrieda has badgered the authorities into allowing Melanie to live with her and be responsible for her good behaviour and so forth.'

'Is she given to this kind of philanthropy?'

'No, this is an entirely new departure. I need hardly tell you that she's deeply involved with every worthwhile charity in the neighbourhood, including the orphanage where Melanie was brought up, but up till now only from a distance.'

'So what's special about Melanie?'

'Oh, she's a character all right. Not to everyone's taste, but I'll leave you to make your own judgement about that. The general opinion is that the most exceptional thing about her is the way she's managed to con Elfrieda.'

'How was it done?'

'Believe it or not, her first coup was to turn up in a laundry basket.'

'I do find it practically unbelievable. How did she manage to do that?'

'Careful calculation, in the view of some people, but I'll give you the story straight. She was on the run from her remand home and found herself outside the theatre just as they were coming out. She's more than slightly stage struck and having kept a special place in her heart for the Rotunda ever since she was taken there as a child to see the pantomime, she had an impulse to nip inside and see what it looked like when the audience had gone home. It's not entirely improbable. You can walk straight on to the stage from the front rows and that's apparently what she did, and got so carried away that she forgot the time. To cut a long story short, she eventually found herself locked in. So, faced with finding somewhere to doss down for the night, she finally made her way to the wardrobe, where she was found fast asleep the next morning. It could all be perfectly true, of course.'

'But what's all this about a remand home? I thought you said she came from an orphanage?'

'Oh yes, indeed, but that was some way back. She ran away from there when she was about fifteen, I gather, and has been in and out of remand homes ever since. In fact, she really has a terrifying record, poor kid, including an illegitimate somewhere along the way, so I'm told. However, she seems to have landed on her feet this time and, if she plays it right, there's no reason why she shouldn't stay on them.'

15

We had reached the main street of Dearehaven by this time, a characterless, modern shopping centre, in complete contrast to the early Victorian residential outskirts and when I remarked on this, Len said bitterly:

'Oh yes, the capitalist speculators have done their best to ruin the place. It used to have a lot of charm in the old days.'

'Did you know it then?'

'No, I didn't,' he said, sounding as though he found the question offensive and adding immediately afterwards:

'Here's your Green Man and, when you're ready to leave, go straight down to the end of this road and you'll come to the Esplanade. Turn right and the theatre's just two minutes away.'

'Thank you, and thanks again for the lift.'

'Don't mention it. And you'll be along in what? Half an hour?'

'Oh, sooner than that. Twenty minutes at the outside.'

'Good! Splendid!' he said, smiling for the first time.

THREE

Predictably enough, the Rotunda Theatre proved to be a circular building with a domed roof and the stage was also in the round, exits and entrances being made by means of ramps at each point of the compass and descending to basement level.

Surrounding it was a steeply raked auditorium holding approximately three hundred people. It was claimed, correctly I believe, that it was possible to see equally well from every seat in the house, so they were unnumbered and all the same price. It was first come first served, thus dispensing with argument or confusion and saving countless man hours for the front-of-house staff.

On the outer perimeter there was another circle, in the form of a wide passage, with bars and cloakrooms set into the back section of it, like jewels on a hooped ring, each with a curved rear wall.

The same motif extended to the outside as well, the building being contained in a small circular walled garden, to which the audience had access before and during performances, and the final touch of rotundity was the office of the Chief Administrator and Licensee, Miss Elfrieda Henshaw. This was situated at the very top of the building, inside the dome, and was approached by a long, winding ramp, somewhat reminiscent of a multi-storey car park.

'No lift, I'm afraid,' Len explained, evidently slightly amused by my rapidly wilting stamina, as we plodded onward and upward. 'There was some engineering problem, I gather. You'll soon get used to it, though. Find yourself skipping up here like a mountain goat in no time.'

'Oh, sure! Doesn't Miss Henshaw find it slightly inconvenient, though?'

'You're joking! She's the only one of us who's not inconvenienced in the least.'

I could only conclude that her living quarters, as well as her office, were housed in this eyrie, but this was only half true. One important fact, which no one had told me, was that Elfrieda suffered from chronic and crippling arthritis and was virtually confined to a wheelchair. Furthermore, it was a highly streamlined machine, custom built and with a kind of outboard motor attached to it, enabling her to scale the heights as easily as she could coast down the slopes.

Being thus equipped gave her a great edge over the people who worked for her, newcomers in particular, for there was no denying that one felt at a distinct psychological disadvantage in having to stagger into her office more or less in the condition of a hundred metre runner who has just breasted the tape.

However, she did unquestionably suffer a good deal of pain, as was evinced by her habit of tightening her lips and frequently placing a hand up to shield her eyes, as well as by the deep lines which grooved her face from her nose to the corners of her mouth.

Without them, she would undoubtedly have been one of the handsomest women ever to go spinning down a ramp in a wheelchair, instead of merely distinguished looking, in a stern and arid kind of way, and I wondered that she should have acquired the reputation of being so plain.

Perhaps the answer was that she had been born at the wrong period, in the wrong place and that in her youth the arbiters of Dearehaven taste had considered tall women with strong features and noble brows to be sadly out of style. So, perhaps in a spirit of defiance, it seemed as though she had gone all out to emphasise her plainness, wearing no make-up, cropping her coarse grey hair with the kitchen scissors, by the look of it, and dressing in clothes which did less than nothing to soften her thin and angular figure. Her complexion was only a shade less grey than her hair, her eyes a pale grey-blue and she looked more like a weary abbot than a female impresario.

Her manner was also rather gauche and she had no aptitude for social chit-chat, her conversation starting off with a few abrupt enquiries about my journey, interspersed with painful silences. This made me nervous, too, and I heard myself yapping on about the magnificence of the room, although, in truth, I was not all that much impressed. It was sparsely and plainly furnished, without flowers, books or ornament of any kind, and the only light coming from the circular skylight in the domed ceiling.

However, it had come as something of a relief to discover that it was not, after all, a perfect circle. It was more the shape of an orange which had one third of it sliced off, having three curved walls and one straight one, facing the door and desk. I was subsequently to learn that when the building had been constructed as a museum and aquarium this dome had housed the library and a special collection of model sailing ships. There had then been two partition walls, dividing the whole into three equal sections. One of them had been left intact during the conversion, in order to provide Elfrieda with her own tiny bedroom and bathroom, so that on first nights and other gala

19

occasions, she could rest and change without leaving the premises.

Fortunately, her uneasiness evaporated as soon as she felt the conventional preliminaries had been adequately dealt with and we had turned to the subject of the play. She then became refreshingly forthright and practical, easily carrying Len along in all her suggestions and comments. Although I felt she was probably right in most of them, it struck me that James Crowther must be a dramatist like no other to leave so many decisions in their hands.

The discussion had lasted for about twenty minutes when Kyril Jones sidled into the room and stood just inside the door, regarding us with a faintly puzzled expression. This was typical behaviour, for I had never seen him when he did not appear to be in a state of disorientation, an impression which was accentuated by his trick of travelling in a vaguely sideways direction, although this may have been an optical illusion, due to one shoulder being hunched a little higher and further forward than the other.

Despite his undistinguished surname, he was a great snob and extremely vain about his noble birth and grand connections, being related, on his mother's side, to practically every living member of the Russian aristocracy and having hosts of princely cousins in Paris, New York and the Earls Court Road. He was also authentically Russian in being extremely inquisitive and opinionated.

The noble blood was always meticulously reflected in his manners and, having advanced further into the room, he bent low over Elfrieda's hand, raising it in a courtly fashion to within an inch of his nose, and was on the point of extending the same treatment to me when, the gesture having brought his face near enough to mine for it to be recognisable, he dropped the old world continental pose and went into paroxysms of silent, shuddering laughter, before patting me gently on the head.

20

'So Kyril has brought our conference to an end,' Elfrieda remarked in a dry, though not ill-humoured tone, 'but I daresay that we have covered all the important points that need to be dealt with at this stage. How about you, Miss Crichton? No worries?'

'None whatever, thank you.'

Looking transparently contrite, Kyril said: 'Oh, but I have interrupted you! How rude and *maladroit*! Forgive me, I beg! I shall go and wait outside until all this is finished. It is twelve-thirty, I think?' he added in a dreamy voice.

'Very nearly,' Elfrieda agreed, glancing at the plain and functional wall clock, which registered twenty-nine minutes past the hour. 'So please stay, Kyril, and let us all have something to eat. I am sure Miss Crichton must be starving.'

This at least was true and I had been speculating from time to time about the contents of various urns and plastic containers which were set out on a table against the partition wall, although even more about the means by which they had arrived there.

'Do you lower baskets through a trapdoor in the floor?' I asked Len who was piling hefty looking sandwiches on to a cardboard plate. Before answering, he put the plate on to a bakelite tray and topped off this dainty repast with a mug of murky looking coffee.

'Not such a bad guess,' he said, pointing to some double doors in the partition wall. 'When I said there was no lift, I'd forgotten about this. It was already installed here, one of those dumb waiter things they used to have in the posh houses. It trundles up and down by pulley between here and the bar.'

'Why does she choose to live this crow's nest life, anyway? Not for the view, because there isn't one. So far as outlook goes, we might just as well be in the basement.'

'You'll be able to understand better when you begin to get to know her,' he replied loftily. 'It's the isolation which appeals. No chance of strangers bursting in on her. You may not have noticed it, but like a good many brilliant and exceptional people, she's amazingly shy. Help yourself to whatever you want and I'll try and join you again when I've delivered this.'

The sandwiches were quite as stodgy and tasteless as they looked and, after sampling a couple and wrapping the remains in a paper napkin which I then dropped in the waste paper basket, I decided to keep my appetite intact for an evening at the Green Man. The scene now in progress round Elfrieda's desk was far more worthy of attention.

About half a dozen more people had congregated there by this time, one of whom in particular caught my attention. Names, all on their own, often conjure up identities to match and, for no better reason than that she was called Melanie, I had pictured a small-boned, winsome creature; sly perhaps, and with a touch of the Pollyanna, but above all ethereal looking. No image could have been further from the reality. She was seated on the corner of Elfrieda's desk, one leg swinging rhythmically and energetically, as though it was unnatural to her ever to be still, a plumpish, bold looking girl, wearing a massive collection of rings, bangles and beads. She had a round, flattish face, sky blue eyes and brilliant carroty red curls. She was wearing a scarlet frilly dress, a daring manoeuvre which had come off surprisingly well, and she was talking her head off, using a lot of expressive and uninhibited gestures and interspersing her chatter with occasional peals of laughter. Everything about her seemed a trifle overdone and yet there was something essentially good humoured in her personality, even at a distance. She radiated a vitality and cheerfulness which literally lighted up those sombre surroundings.

It evidently affected Elfrieda in the same way, for she was leaning back in her wheelchair, listening to every word, with an expression of amused affectionate tolerance, which quite transformed the normal harsh set of her face. It was not hard to see why the company in general so resented this earthy, alien interloper in their exclusive circle and the easy way in which she monopolised the queen bee.

Probably one of the few to feel no jealousy on this score was Kyril, who now came sidling up to the table and began a slow inspection and appraisal of the sandwiches. In this, as in all his movements, there was a sleepiness more readily associated with the drone than the worker bee, but I knew from experience that, so far as his career was concerned, this was deceptive.

'So that's Melanie?' I asked him, still watching her.

'Yes, Melanie,' he replied in a mournful tone, giving the name a French intonation, which made it sound even more spiritual. 'How much you have learnt already, Tessa! *C'est étonnant!* Len told you, I suppose?'

'Yes, and so you are not so *étonné*, after all? He seems to have quite an obsession about her?'

Kyril gave me a wolfish grin, showing a lot of white, uneven teeth:

'He is always apprehensive, poor Len. Very sensitive and highly strung, you know. *Pauvre garçon.*'

'And has he any reason to be afraid of Melanie?'

'Perhaps. She is the unknown quantity, you might say. Elfrieda has some strong maternal instincts, I believe, which were stifled until she was quite an old woman. Then she found this great big round shoe and filled it with all her children, making us work hard and come when we were called, but still it was not enough. Some of the children

23

were quite grown up and a few of us were so naughty as to have minds of our own. But now she has found somebody who is very nearly a real daughter to her and that is bound to cause some sparks.'

He spoke so softly that I had difficulty in catching every word, but, as Len had pointed out, the gist was clear enough and I took another, more critical look at the subject of our conversation. It told me nothing, however, because she now had her back to us and was seated at the desk, head bent and bejewelled left arm stretched out across it, as she wrote from Elfrieda's dictation. All the others had now moved away and Len caught my eye and beckoned me over to join them.

They included a young man and a middle-aged woman, who were introduced to me as Jack Henderson and Jill Sandford, a coincidence which I gathered from Len's expression merited a trill of amusement, and they were A.S.M. and Stage Manager respectively. What secretly amused me though was how, quite apart from their names, they complemented each other so perfectly. He was a delicate looking boy, with tiny hands and feet, almost girlish in physique, and she was a large, raw-boned muscular looking woman, who looked as though she could have flung him across the room with one hand. They were both friendly, in an offhand, abstracted kind of way and soon left us and went into a private huddle round the sandwich table.

Number three was a sharp featured girl, with beautiful eyes, named Janice, who was also in the cast and finally there was Viola Hopkins, who was at present appearing in two of the current productions and was to play my mother-in-law in the forthcoming one.

Although this was our first personal encounter, I had seen Viola a number of times during her career, which had taken an unusual, although not unique course. In her youth she had possessed neither looks nor ability above the average, she was tall and on the fat side, which was limiting for her and had never been known to give a performance which could be rated higher than competent. Nevertheless, she was consistently in work in supporting roles in rep. and on provincial tours and it was said that most of these came her way because of her ability to get along well with people and to work hard and unselfishly in any part she was offered.

However, after some dozen or fifteen years of this slog, she had turned up at the Rotunda, playing a series of middle-aged and elderly parts, well before her time, and it soon became apparent that this was the niche which had been kept vacant for her and which, with no upsurge of talent, but a great deal of hard-won experience, she was able to fill to perfection. She was now in her fourth successive season there and was in constant demand during the rest of the year in films and television, living proof of Elfrieda's much quoted genius for bringing out latent or unrecognised talent in those who worked with her.

I was pleased to find that this run of success had not gone to her head. She was unaffectedly friendly and welcoming and further endeared herself by going into transports of praise, on learning where I was staying, for the genius of Mr and Mrs Banks in the matter of dishing up lobster and crab, not to mention my own cleverness in discovering them.

The slightly overpowering sensation of being surrounded by so much plain living and high thinking was agreeably lightened by this descent into the materialist world and I was rather annoyed by Melanie's choosing this moment to interrupt us. She did not do so rudely, by breaking into our conversation, but stationed herself beside us, making it clear that she did not intend to go away.

'Something you want, Melanie?' Viola asked, not un-kindly, but with a hint of irritability.

'Miss Henshaw asked me to give this to Miss Crichton,' Melanie replied, handing me a sheet of writing paper.

She had quite a pleasant, if over-loud voice, with a slight regional accent and sounded completely self-assured and at ease.

'Oh, thank you,' I said. 'What is it?'

'Well, you see, Miss Henshaw guessed you'd be looking for digs while you're down here, so she got me to write out these addresses for you. She said to tell you they're all places she can recommend personally.'

'How very thoughtful of her! Thank you.'

'That's okay. All part of the Rotunda service,' Melanie said, the suggestion of pertness in this remark modified, rather than accentuated by the broad wink which accom-panied it.

'It really is most thoughtful and kind,' I said to Viola, looking down at the three addresses, 'but oh dear, oh dear!'

'What's the trouble?'

'Hard to explain without sounding ungrateful, but I'd rather planned on finding something a little further away from my place of work. I confess to finding something a bit stifling and cradle-to-the-grave about it. No offence meant.'

'And none taken, my dear, I understand perfectly; but if that's how you feel you'd better come and share with me. I've rented the dinkiest little house, perched high up on the cliff. It's two miles out from the town and has the most glorious views you've ever seen. Green hills at the back and your actual blue sea in front. Some of the time, anyway.'

'Sounds bliss, but have you got room for me?'

'Shall have, by the time you come. Lawrence, my current

lodger, has a three months' tour coming up. Anyway, why not come for a drink this evening and see what you think of the place? I can collect you from your pub on my way home.'

'You are an angel, Viola! It sounds marvellous and it's terribly kind of you!'

'Not a bit. I don't particularly enjoy life in the country on my own and Larry can't really afford his share of the rent when he's not using it, so it would be doing us all a good turn. Besides, you may be able to give me a few tips.'

'Me? Give tips to you?' I asked in astonishment.

'Oh, not professional, although I'm sure you could do that too. I was thinking of your secondary activity, your heavy connections with the world of crime.'

'However did you hear about that?'

'A cousin of yours is an old friend of mine. Toby Crichton.'

'Yes, I remember now. You were in a play of his about five years ago, weren't you?'

'That's right. The most lazy, selfish and abominable man who ever lived and I simply adore him.'

'He simply adores you too,' I hastened to tell her, although unable to remember whether he did or not. 'So what tips do you need of a criminal nature?'

'Oh, nothing complicated. Just the basic rules for committing the perfect murder will do to be going on with.'

Curiously enough, this was by no means the first time I had been asked for this advice and I decided to vary the monotony for myself by giving her a straight answer.

'There is no universal rule,' I told her. 'Everything depends on the personality of the intended victim.'

'Does it now?' she asked, looking somewhat taken aback. 'Why is that?'

'Well, you see, Viola, most people carry the seeds of their own destruction inside themselves. They drive too fast, or drink too much, or are chronically absent-minded. It could be one of a dozen quite trivial weaknesses and what you have to do is to concentrate on whichever one he or she is most vulnerable to and capitalise on it.'

'My word!' Viola said with a laugh no longer quite so merry. 'So Toby wasn't joking, after all! I hadn't expected my innocent little quip to be taken quite so seriously, but I can see that you're an expert on the subject and I can't wait to hear more. Not this evening, though.'

'Why not?'

'Because Jamie Crowther will be with us and he has a nervous disposition. We don't want to upset him with this kind of talk, do we? Not if we know what's good for us.'

I agreed that in these circumstances it would be wiser to postpone further discussion of the subject until we were alone, but in fact she never referred to it again.

FOUR

Until then, my acquaintance with James Crowther had been limited to a very few, very brief and impersonal meetings at first night parties and suchlike, but, although there was nothing in his behaviour to bear it out, it had come as no surprise to hear that he was a nervous type. In my experience, nearly all playwrights are martyrs to neurosis in one form or another and some of them run the whole gamut, the claustrophobia no sooner having been brought under control than some blunt and unsympathetic review sets off the suicidal depression.

My cousin Toby, whose annual output averages about half a play and a couple of television scripts, is equally a prey to such moods and obsessions, haunted not only by desperate insecurity about his own work, but by the conviction that even his most obscure rivals will inevitably be recognised as possessing a far greater talent.

Jamie, at this time, was about forty-five, tall and rather stout as well, which was curious considering how much weight punishing exercise he took. He had small, dark, inquisitive eyes and jet black hair which looked as though it had been painted on to his head. His private life verged on the reclusive, but his public one was a matter of intimate knowledge and concern to many thousands on both sides of the Atlantic, who counted it a poor year which went by without at least one new Crowther comedy. In fact, during his association with the Rotunda there had been no less than eight major successes, all of them having transferred to London and Broadway after the Deare-haven season.

They neither were nor aimed to be in any way memorable or profound, but the formula was unbeatable: tautly constructed plots, sharp characterisation, an innate sense of the theatre and the magic gift of being able to make people laugh.

He was also a man of diverse talents, as I now discovered and was currently in the process of re-covering all his dining room chairs in petit point, from a design which he had created himself. For convenience' sake he kept one canvas permanently at Viola's cottage, so that he could tear straight into it whenever he called there.

However, the fact that none of this had helped to over-come the insubstantial fears to which people of his calling are so prone was evidenced by the way he instantly started to cross-examine me on Toby's current activities, whether, in particular, he was at work on a play or, worse still, had one ready to go into production. Having already come under Viola's influence, I felt it only prudent to reassure him on both counts, explaining that many weeks had passed since Toby had felt inspired to take up his pen for anything more momentous than a letter to the Parish Magazine and, furthermore, was becoming resigned to the fact that his small stock of inspiration had now dried up, leaving him more or less in the position of a sucked orange.

All this cheered Jamie up wonderfully and he then became very buoyant and genial, which one could not help feeling was the role for which Nature had fashioned him, only throwing in the writing talent and its attendant curses as a careless afterthought, for it was plain that, alongside the moody blues, there existed quite another personality which was notable for its enjoyment of the good things of life. The good things on this occasion included half a bottle of the most expensive champagne on the market and it occurred to me that since he was obviously a frequent visitor this must make serious inroads on the housekeeping budget. However, when I mentioned it later to Viola, she assured me that a similar arrangement was in force here as with the needlework and that she received a regular weekly delivery from his own wine merchant.

There being nothing like champagne for making the party go, the three of us soon became very convivial, exchanging theatrical news and gossip, with Viola bringing us up to date on recent developments at the Rotunda and Jamie throwing off a series of hilarious imitations, including a particularly clever one of Elfrieda.

'Were you ever an actor?' I asked him.

'Yes, for a short time. An appallingly bad one too.'

'Oh no, surely?'

'Oh yes, indeed, my darling, I have no illusions there. It was valuable experience, as it turned out, but one of the sad truths is that good mimics are not much good for anything else. I could give you a fair impression of any lord or knight you care to name in the part of Hamlet, but I could no more play Hamlet myself than go for a walk on the moon.'

There was no telling whether this was an intentionally malicious observation, but it was certainly wanting in tact, for on the drive up to her cottage Viola had also revealed herself to be an excellent mimic. However, her impersonations, although funny, managed to be kindly and gentle as well, which was certainly not always true of Jamie's, as he then proceeded to demonstrate, achieving a positive *tour de force* as he reeled off passages from the Queen

31

Mab speech in three distinct, immediately recognisable styles. He was on the third of these when there was an interruption which abruptly brought the curtain down on this merry scene. Len appeared on the terrace, wearing the mask of tragedy and more or less wringing his hands.

He waved away offers of champagne, saying he preferred beer, if you don't mind, and sank down into a deck chair.

'My dear boy, is something the matter?' Jamie asked, looking up from his tapestry with mild concern.

'You can say that again! And again! Elfrieda's had an inspiration.'

'Oh, that's nice! And what are we all going to be doing now?'

'You're not going to like this, Jamie, but she said I was to be the one to break it to you, so here I am, breaking it.'

'What am I not going to like?'

'She wants Melanie to do Rosie.'

'Rosie? You mean my schoolgirl?'

'Right.'

'Am I losing my hearing, or are you actually telling me that she wants Melanie to have the part?'

'Well, she wants you to hear Melanie read it. I suppose you'd consent to that?'

'Then you suppose wrong. Melanie can read it in Sanskrit, standing on her head and dressed up as Charles the Second, for all I care. It won't do her the slightest good.'

'The problem is that I'm afraid Elfrieda has rather set her heart on it.'

'Then her heart must be set off it again. I never heard a more outrageous proposal in my life. Has she gone raving mad? Apart from everything else, we'd settled that Janice should do it and Elfrieda was the first to agree that she'd be very good.'

'Yes, I know,' Len said, now looking close to tears, 'but,

32

if you remember, that was before Melanie came on the scene.'

'Well, she won't appear in any scene of mine, I'll tell you that much. You'll have to be firm, Len; make her understand that it's quite out of the question.'

'And when did you last try being firm with Elfrieda?'

'Never. You know perfectly well that it's not my policy to interfere. On the other hand, we have a tacit agreement that my wishes should be consulted at every stage in the game and that she would never, in any circumstances, go against them. It saves a lot of time and argument and it has always worked perfectly. It is up to you to ensure that the arrangement continues.'

Viola, who had been looking quite as put out as the other two, now produced one of the peacemaking compromises for which she was so justly famous:

'It's a very small part, Jamie. How about if Melanie were to understudy?'

'Nothing at all about it. Any fool could guess what would happen, if I were to allow that. Elfrieda would get to work with her pins and wax and on the first night Janice would be stricken with the full laryngitis. I'm not falling into that trap, thank you very much.'

'Has she any experience at all?' I asked, this having become a game in which everyone could join.

'Apart from Buttons in the Orphanage production of Cinders, not as far as I know.'

'Then how . . . ?'

'Has Elfrieda managed to hit on this quaint idea? One asks oneself! Perhaps not being a professional herself, she doesn't see the need for anyone else to be. Anyway, there it is,' he said, getting up. 'You know my views, Len, and you must pass them on to her with all speed. I am simply not having it and that's final.'

33

'I just hope she'll take it, that's all,' Len said in a doom laden mumble.

'It is up to you to see that she does, my dear. Otherwise, I'm warning you, there's going to be trouble. Goodnight, Viola sweetheart. Sorry to be so sour, but there are limits, aren't there? Goodness me, how petty this little world of ours can get sometimes, don't you agree?'

With which heretical words, he turned his back and stalked off across the garden.

Viola was unusually quiet on the drive back to Dearehaven and her expression unusually forbidding. It forbade me quite successfully for the first mile and a half and then, curiosity once more overcoming discretion, I asked:

'Who'll win?'

'Just what I've been wondering.'

'What's the precedent?'

'There hasn't been one. That's what makes the situation so odd. I suppose some clash was bound to come eventually, with two such iron willed characters, but up till now they've always had each other's measure and Elfrieda seems to have known instinctively just how far she could go and when to give in gracefully.'

'So perhaps she will this time?'

'One can only hope so.'

'Although Len didn't seem very optimistic.'

'No, and he's the last person to work on her; far too emotional, for a start, and he's completely starry-eyed about Elfrieda. Well, most of them are, I suppose, but Len is also terrified about his own job, which makes him quite unfit to take her on.'

'So stalemate?'

'I should think so, with the line they're pursuing at the moment. The unfortunate truth is that if Melanie sees this as her big chance to become a star overnight, then

34

Elfrieda is likely to make sure she gets it, however absurd and unacceptable the idea may be to the rest of us. Don't ask me why she's got this obsession or infatuation, or whatever it is, but it's stupid and pointless to ignore it.'

'I won't ask you why, because I think I can guess?'

'Indeed? And what is your guess?'

'For a start, Melanie reminds her of herself when young.'

'Oh, really?' Viola asked, looking highly amused. 'A podgy, red-headed urchin from a remand home? I wouldn't have called the similarities very obvious.'

'Not in their appearance or background, I agree, except that they've probably both suffered from being considered hopelessly plain by their contemporaries. But they also both possess this burning passion for the theatre and it is probably just as difficult for a penniless orphan to break in as it was for an ungainly girl from a rich, puritanical family. In a sense, Elfrieda is getting her vicarious revenge against all the people who blighted her own youth.'

'The only difference being that Elfrieda's passion, if slightly dotty, is at least genuine.'

'And you don't think that's true of Melanie?'

'I've yet to be convinced of it,' Viola replied. 'I could be wrong, of course, but in my book she's no more than a shrewd little opportunist, sharp enough to have hit on the right formula to get her hands on everything that's going.'

'If so, she's not only shrewd, she's a positive genius. I think, you see, Viola, that she is using another weapon which is even stronger than the others. I was watching Elfrieda when Melanie was perched on her desk, giggling and chatting. She was listening to every word and she looked really human, almost fond and foolish, you might say, and I shouldn't be surprised if that's where the real secret lies. During the first part of her life, Elfrieda was bullied and frustrated and now she gets awe and respect from all sides; but she's probably never known what it is to be on equal terms with anyone. And now along comes Melanie, who gives her affection and gratitude, but is quite irreverent; treats her, in fact, like any other jolly old auntie. It must make a change, to say the least.'

'My word, you do have a sharp eye for the human foibles, don't you, Tessa? I can see I shall have to watch my step.'

'No, you won't, and personally I can't see that it makes much difference whether Melanie is genuine and sincere or not. So long as Elfrieda believes in her, doesn't it amount to the same thing?'

'Yes, there I do agree with you; and, as I mentioned before, if the wretched girl is really set on making a fool of herself in public, Elfrieda will be there to see that she does. Which is why I consider that Jamie is going quite the wrong way about it.'

'What is the alternative?'

'Obviously, someone must persuade Melanie that this is not what she wants at all. Simple as that.'

I agreed that this would be the happiest solution of all, though unable to see how it could be achieved any more easily than the other.

FIVE

Rehearsals for the new Crowther play, which was called *Au Pair*, were scheduled to begin on Tuesday, 20th May and the previous Sunday was notable for the fact that when the telephone rang, in what can only have been a mood of deep abstraction, Toby answered it himself.

'Hallo!' I heard him say. 'Yes, it is . . . Rather tired, but otherwise all right, thank you. And you? No, I'm afraid I can't tell you where she is. She could be upstairs in her room, or in the garden, or a dozen places, you know how restless the young are? . . . Yes, that's right, and Robin too, both here . . . but he's playing golf.'

Unable to contain my curiosity any longer, I went into the hall and, with an expression of profound relief, he handed over the receiver.

'Viola,' he explained, 'babbling on about having tried to ring you in London, though goodness knows why, since you're so soon to be living in each other's pockets. And it beats me why you don't get an answering service.'

'Robin is against it,' I replied. 'He doesn't see why we should go to all that trouble just to make life easier for the burglars. Hallo, Viola!'

'Stunning news,' I announced, returning to the drawing

room after another ten minutes. 'Melanie has swiped the petty cash and scarpered.'

'The delinquent orphan?'

'That's the one. Isn't it staggering, though?'

'Not particularly. She didn't sound like a very stable character.'

'She's had no incentive to be stable up till now, but having met her and heard of her reputation, I must say that staggered is the word for what I am. She really had it made with Elfrieda. Anyone could see that the old lady was potty about her and what a fool to throw all that away for a few mouldy pounds.'

'Is that literally all?'

'No, to be accurate, a nice round fifty. Elfrieda made out the cheque and gave it to Jill to cash, which is the regular practice, but on this occasion Melanie happened to be present and she offered to do it. It seems she was about to set forth for her driving lesson and she said she could easily drop into the bank on her way home.'

'And then forgot to come back with the money, I take it?'

'Never got to the lesson either. Just drew the money and vanished. Viola's dancing on air, needless to say. She'd just got back from London, heard the news and couldn't wait to pass it on.'

'When did it happen, then?'

'Friday morning, although it was several hours before anyone really noticed. Apparently, these driving instructors are apt to be rather flexible when there's an attractive girl behind the wheel and she often got extra time. At least Viola says Melanie always made this her excuse when she was late back, although not necessarily true.'

'Easy enough to check, I should have thought?'

'Except that why should anyone have bothered to, since the longer she stayed out of sight the better they liked it? All except Elfrieda, of course, and she's still insisting that her precious lamb is innocent. Whether she actually believes it or is simply too proud to admit she's been bamboozled, is anyone's guess.'

'Both attitudes equally shaky, I should have thought, in view of the small matter of the missing fifty pounds. Or does she favour the theory that the girl was mugged as she came out of the bank and is even now lying unconscious in some dark alley?'

'They don't have dark alleys in Dearehaven and, on the contrary, Elfrieda maintains that the cheque was never cashed. She says that when she telephoned the bank they told her it hadn't been presented. No one believes that for a second, I might add. They assume that Elfrieda is more than willing to wave goodbye to fifty quid, as a face saver, and cheap at the price.'

'And which version do you believe?'

'Ah, well you see, I haven't quite made up my mind yet. It's true that all of them know both characters far more intimately than I do and should be in a better position to judge, and yet . . .'

'You think they're most likely wrong?'

'It's complicated by the fact that her disappearance at this stage is undeniably very convenient for them, and perhaps even for Elfrieda as well. She may have been having second thoughts about the wisdom of antagonising everyone by pushing Melanie into the part, but too proud to climb down and admit her mistake. Then there's Jamie, isn't there? He's a devious man, I shouldn't wonder, and if he'd realised that nothing was going to budge Elfrieda, he might have changed his tactics. I remember Viola remarking that they were attacking the problem from the wrong direction and the subtle thing would be to persuade Melanie to give up the part of her own accord.'

'And what persuasion could have been used to bring that about?'

'Money, presumably; and, if so, it could possibly be true that the cheque was never cashed. Melanie may not have needed to take that risk. Elfrieda is not the only one at the Rotunda with that sort of money to fling about. Perhaps they all chipped in? I'll have to try and sort it out when I get there.'

'It's a relief to know that you're not going to die of boredom in Dearehaven,' Toby said. 'As mysteries go, this one must strike you as rather tame, but at least you can use it to keep your hand in and provide yourself with a little harmless diversion.'

As it happened, though, it was to provide numerous other people, as well as myself, with a good deal more than that.

SIX

This time there was no one to meet me at Dorchester and I underwent my first experience of travelling backwards along the twenty miles of branch line. I was on the last of the six coaches, all crowded with passengers, many of them parents with children and weighed down with buckets and spades and shrimping nets.

This gave rise to a certain amount of risk and discomfort, particularly when we disembarked on to the Dearehaven platform and were herded into a tight throng round the ticket collector. I was too busy protecting my legs and my luggage to pay much attention to individuals, but on looking up at one moment to assess the numbers still ahead of me, I had a brief glimpse of one just passing through the gate. We were separated by at least thirty other people and she had her back to me, but the height matched, and so did the dress and hair. So it seemed that, after all, I was to be denied my one small diversion.

'No, no,' Viola said firmly, 'she has most certainly not come back and I should be very surprised to learn that she is not already a hundred miles away. You must have been mistaken, Tessa. The police would have caught up with her long ago if she were anywhere near Dearehaven.'

'So it's a police matter, is it?'

'Had to be. I feel sure Elfrieda was highly reluctant to bring them in, but technically Melanie is still on probation. Not even the great and glorious Miss Henshaw could get round that one.'

'So what's the position now?'

'No change. She's officially registered as a missing person and that's most likely how it will stay. They think she may have headed for London, which is the easiest place of all to get lost in; but she could be absolutely anywhere; on the beach at Blackpool or walking the streets of Bristol. With fifty pounds in her pocket, plus a few other small sums she's probably nicked off Elfrieda in her time, it wouldn't be too difficult to disappear and I very much doubt if she'll be bothering us again.'

'Jamie must be pleased as punch?'

'No doubt he is. Things were coming to a right old pass there, with him threatening to dissociate himself publicly with the production and Elfrieda still flatly refusing to back down. It's quite the nicest thing that could have happened, from his point of view, but naturally he's far too canny to admit it or to do any crowing. In fact, he's being ultra charming and tactful, behaving as though Melanie's departure were a great loss to us all and no doubt keeping his fingers crossed that it is one we shall have to learn to live with.'

'I wouldn't bank on it.'

'And I still say you're wrong. It couldn't possibly have been her you saw. Our local clodhoppers may not be in Robin's class when it comes to the big stuff, but they'd be perfectly capable of sorting out a girl like Melanie, who happens to be one they know only too well already, if she showed her face in Dearehaven.'

This conversation took place on Monday evening, a few hours after my arrival. We were sitting on the verandah of Viola's dinky cottage, high up on the cliff to the east of Dearehaven, which we could see spread out below and to the left of us. There was a similar and equally steep cliff head on the far side of it and the wide bay between them looked as though it had literally been scooped out of the chalk by some neat and purposeful hand.

Toby had been quite horrified by my description of the cottage and its surroundings because he has a phobia about heights, among numerous others, and is apt to suffer from giddy spells while looking at the stage from the front row of the dress circle, but in fact at no point did one have the sense of being thus perched up high on a promontory, still less of the nearby two hundred foot drop from the edge of the cliff to the beach below. Not even the tide line was visible, only a vast expanse of sea, with little boats dotted about on it, a patch or two of white froth where waves broke over a ridge of high rocks and an occasional steam ship almost stationary on the horizon.

The reason for this false sense of security was that the cottage was set about fifty yards back from the cliff edge, with a strip of garden in front of it, enclosed by a high hedge whose main components seemed to be gorse and bramble. There were a few scruffy, neglected flower beds and some lumps of chalk in one corner, where someone had once started to make a rock garden, but the soil was obviously one to dishearten the most enthusiastic gardener and Viola had made no attempt to put it in order.

Still further to the east, some quarter of a mile away in the direction of the golf course, stood the large and solid Edwardian villa, the property of Jamie Crowther, separated from its only neighbour by a large garden and stretch of common land. This gave him the privacy he prized so highly, as well as plenty of opportunity for solitary exercise. He spent half his days tramping about the countryside and thought nothing of walking down to Dearehaven and back. Most of his creative inspiration, so he claimed, came to him during these lonely marches and many of his social comings and goings were also conducted on foot.

It was no accident that he had been present when I first visited Viola's cottage, for she had explained afterwards that he enjoyed companionship in small doses and on his own terms, but only with a chosen few and that, although she was rarely invited to his house, where he led a bachelor and reclusive life, he made a regular practice of walking over to hers on any evening when she was not needed at the theatre.

She did not seem to resent this one-sided arrangement in the least, which was probably a wise and sensible attitude, and, this being Monday when she had no performance, the champagne had been on ice all day, his favourite chair placed between us, with the bag containing canvas, thimble and wool, on a table beside it. No doubt, it was precisely this kind of thoughtful attention which had done so much to advance her career to its present level.

At ten minutes after six he duly came stamping round the side of the house to avail himself of this charming hospitality and, as soon as his immediate needs had been attended to, Viola launched into a secondhand, although accurate description of my vision at the railway station. This at least indicated that she genuinely believed it to be a case of mistaken identity, for I felt sure that it was not in her nature to pass on unwelcome news, if she believed there was any truth in it. If so, she must have been badly taken aback by Jamie's response.

'Has Elfrieda been told about this?' he asked, flashing his shrewd and sharp brown eyes from one to the other of us.

44

'Why no, my dear, certainly not. I've only just heard about it myself and I've no intention of repeating it to anyone else. It would be madness to stir things up again and raise false hopes in that quarter. I am sure you agree?'

He did not, however, and did not hesitate to say so.

'But, my dear Jamie, what possible good could it do?'

'The point is that I have a nasty feeling that some similar tale may already have reached her ears, or will soon do so.'

'Why do you say that?'

'Because, my dearest Viola, another of my nasty feelings is that Tessa is probably right.'

'You can't be serious?'

'I can, you know, and for the excellent reason that, although until five minutes ago I was ready to pass it off as hallucination or a waking nightmare, I now feel fairly certain that I saw Melanie too.'

'Jamie! Are you serious? When and where?'

'This afternoon. I was on my way back from the golf course and when I got up here, on to level ground, I saw this creature bouncing along ahead of me. The sun was in my eyes and she was quite fifty yards away, so I couldn't swear to it, but it struck me at once that there was quite an uncanny resemblance. Naturally, I hadn't intended to say a word about it. To do so, as you say, would only cause trouble and I could so easily have been mistaken. However, since she now appears to be flaunting around all over the place, it can only be a matter of hours before Elfrieda gets to hear about it. We must keep our little fingers crossed that the full disillusionment will have set in by now, but I wouldn't depend on it.'

'But Melanie must be half-witted if she thinks she can get away with it,' Viola protested. 'And somehow that doesn't add up. I thought she was a shrewd little schemer, with her eye firmly on the ball.'

'How did you recognise her?' I asked Jamie. 'Was it her hair?'

'Not particularly, although the red dress struck me as horridly familiar, and also the bulging carrier bag; but I think the chief thing was her gait. You remember that rather coltish way of moving? Quite distinctive and not unattractive in its way. Her legs looked as though they had springs inside them.'

'Why ever didn't you catch her up and find out for certain?' Viola asked, sounding aggrieved about it.

'Partly from reluctance to have my worst fears confirmed, partly because it could so easily have been embarrassing. She wasn't alone, you see.'

'Oh?'

'She had a young man with her, a fair haired youth in blue jeans. I didn't recognise him at all, but Melanie, if it was she, had obviously struck up a firm friendship. They were swinging along, hand in hand. I should have felt rather silly if I'd come panting up behind them to peer into their faces and been confronted by a couple of complete strangers. Anyway, they disappeared down that footpath to the beach, so I let it go and tried to put the whole thing out of my mind.'

'All the same,' Viola said, frowning, 'oughtn't the police to be warned?'

'If I were you, my dear, I'd lie low and not interfere. There's a good chance that if the dear girl is still in our midst, the police know all about it and to have their attention called to it officially would only be an embarrassment.'

'I must be stupid,' Viola said, 'because I simply do not follow you. If they do know, why do they allow her to wander around on the loose? Surely the practical thing would be to pick her up and pop her back in the remand home?'

'From which Elfrieda would retrieve her in no time at all, thus starting the whole boring business up again. I can't see that as a very satisfactory solution and I daresay they don't either. You have to remember that since Elfrieda remains adamant on the subject of her cheque and would undoubtedly refuse to prosecute, technically the only crime Melanie has committed is in breaking the probation rules. That wouldn't earn her a very stiff sentence.'

'Ah, I do begin to see now what you're driving at. And, from that rather smug expression on Tessa's face, I have a nasty feeling that she got there first.'

'Crime is my hobby,' I told her. 'I've had more experience of it than you.'

'It's true, is it?' Jamie asked. 'Kyril said something about it, but I didn't know whether to believe him or not. However, I daresay you agree with me that this must be the answer to the mystery?'

'I wonder, though? Would the police really be so devious, simply to protect Elfrieda from her own altruism?'

'That is probably a secondary motive and I can think of a far more practical one. Melanie has proved herself to be quite a little nuisance, one way and another, so they intend to sit tight, keeping an unobtrusive watch on her activities, in the belief that she is bound to land herself in real trouble sooner or later. At which point, if we're lucky, they'll be able to crack down and put her away, safely out of Elfrieda's reach and all our lives for at least a year.'

Jamie uttered this prediction with serene confidence, which I personally considered misplaced and, in fact, nothing could have been more wildly over-optimistic.

SEVEN

The first read-through of *Au Pair* began at ten o'clock on Tuesday morning and continued, without a hitch, until one, when we broke for lunch, Len reminding us to be back in an hour for the afternoon session.

I noticed that Janice, who had been recalled to the cast at twenty-four hours' notice, was already well versed in the schoolgirl part, which indicated either an exceptional memory, or an unshakeable faith that her luck would turn. However, observing her sharp little face and listening to her rather tinny voice, I was struck by the notion that Elfrieda might have shown more insight than she had been given credit for in insisting that Melanie should replace her.

For a start, Janice was at least ten years too old and, although make-up and a change of hair style could obviously do wonders for her appearance, there was a maturity in her figure and movements, which I felt sure would always betray her. She was not nearly experienced enough to disguise the fact that she was an adult and not a gawky adolescent. Melanie, on the other hand, was almost the real thing and this could not have failed to enhance both the comedy and the pathos which Jamie had written into the character. With good direction and only a little natural talent, it could have been inspired casting and I was surprised that he should have set his face so firmly against it, without troubling to find out whether she was suitable or not.

During the lunch break Kyril sidled up and asked me how it was going.

'Pretty well, so far,' I assured him. 'I think Len knows what he's doing. I was afraid he'd have us all playing it as the fish-and-chip brigade on a package tour from Birmingham, and it's not that sort of play, but there hasn't been a hint of it, I'm thankful to say.'

'You should not worry about such things,' Kyril said, patting my shoulder. 'These proletarian attitudes are something of a pose. He would not be such a fool as to let them influence his artistry.'

'As I am beginning to realise.'

'He has a big chip on the shoulder, that one, and it takes an amusing form. You know, he is not such a working class boy as he would wish us to believe. His father was a pharmacist, I believe, but you mustn't say I told you and you must pretend not to know.'

'Honestly, Kyril, it amazes me how you dig out these scandalous secrets.'

This caused him to shake with silent laughter and, when he had recovered, he asked me if I would care to take an aperitif at his flat that evening and cast an eye over his model for the set. I accepted at once because his designs were invariably imaginative and original and I was particularly interested to see what he had done with this one. Jamie had allowed for only one set which, except for lighting and props, remained unchanged throughout, but it was a complicated one, on two levels, the façade of a villa in Cyprus, containing a pair of furnished flats

49

which separate English families, formerly unknown to each other, had rented for their summer holidays. Part of the action took place on the terrace outside the ground floor flat, part on the balcony of the one above and some on both simultaneously. So it would require ingenuity, as well as technical expertise.

'I would like to very much,' I told him, 'but only if you can lay on a taxi to take me home afterwards.'

'But of course, *chérie*. In fact, I shall drive you myself.'

'That's kind of you! I'll simply have to do something about hiring a car. I can't always rely on other people for lifts.'

'Perhaps Elfrieda could help you with that problem,' Kyril said, with one of his wolfish grins.

'Oh really? Don't tell me she's in the car hire business too?'

'No, but she may have a secondhand one to dispose of. It is improbable that she will have much use for it now.'

This remark recalled something Len had told me at our first meeting and I said:

'Oh, I see! She bought it for Melanie?'

'Yes, and driving lessons to go with it. What an imbecile to throw it all away, wasn't she, for such a mess of potage as fifty pounds?'

'Absolutely daft, I agree. One could understand it, up to a point, if she were finding her new life rather a strain and decided the time had come to move on, but if it's true that she's still prowling around Dearehaven, it makes no sense at all.'

'Why do you say she is still in Dearehaven?' Kyril asked with such untypical sharpness that he quite made me jump.

'At least two people claim to have seen her and I am one of them.'

'Where?'

'At the railway station. I could have been mistaken, though,' I added, for I was beginning to regret having brought the subject up. It was not that I had been sworn to secrecy or felt any obligation to suppress the news, but the eager way in which Kyril had pounced on it, so different from his normal lethargic responses, was making me uneasy. To get away from the subject, I said:

'Perhaps I won't talk to her about the car just now. Something tells me that it wouldn't go down very well.'

'No, she is not very approachable these days.'

'And she looks dreadfully ill. Don't you think so?'

'I don't know. I didn't notice anything particularly bad while I was talking to her and she always has the face of someone who is nearly dead. Is it worse today? I can't see very clearly from this distance.'

'Terribly tired and drawn looking. As though she hadn't slept for a week.'

'Well, that's nothing, *ma chère*. She very often doesn't sleep; although I think things were better when you came here the first time. Perhaps the naughty girl so tired her out that even with all that pain she could not keep awake at night. You are seeing her now in her normal state and anyone else would have been dead years ago. I shall go and cheer her up. Don't forget this evening. I'll be waiting outside for you at six o'clock. And, if I should run into a certain person perhaps I shall invite her to join us.'

Pausing only to help himself to another sandwich, he ambled away, his shoulders hunched and heaving with mirth as though he had just made the funniest joke in the world.

The rehearsal continued throughout the afternoon and during the latter part of it we were joined by the author. He sat quietly and unobtrusively in a corner of the room, scarcely lifting his eyes from the script, but making copious

51

notes as we went along and I noticed that, little by little, Len's composure deserted him. He rarely looked directly at Jamie, pretending indeed to be almost unaware of his presence. Clearly, though, it was only a pretence, for his eyes frequently strayed obliquely in that direction, reminding me of someone in a studio audience who has been warned not to look at the camera, and he became increasingly fidgety and forgetful, losing his place and losing his grip as well. I could only trust that Jamie had recognised the demoralising effect he was having and did not intend to make a regular habit of it.

We broke at five-thirty, with sighs of relief from all sides, but fresh trouble was awaiting us, literally just around the corner. Not for nothing had our round house once housed an aquarium, for we could just as well have been fishes swimming around in a tank ourselves for all we knew of conditions in the world outside. On this particular afternoon they had changed in a dramatic fashion and, attired as I was in the cotton slacks and sandals which had been so appropriate when I set out in the morning, it was a nasty shock on reaching the stage door to find that the alleyway outside had been transformed into a shallow river, with the rain still beating down on to it like a deluge of soluble pebbles.

Several other people in the same plight were peering dismally out through the half open door, among them Viola and Jamie, although there was no sign of Kyril.

'He must have left before this started,' Viola said, in answer to my enquiries. 'Trust Kyril! I'd offer you a lift, but I can't even get to my car until it lets up a bit. Do you want to hang on?'

'No, it's all right, thank you, I'll get a taxi.'

Len was inside the stage door keeper's office, speaking on the house phone.

'You'll be lucky,' he said, putting his receiver down,

when, having consulted a list pinned to the wall, I began to dial Dearehaven Cabs Ltd. 'Quite apart from the fact that they all go home for tea the minute there's a drop of rain about, this happens to be the business man's commuting time and all the best pickings are at the railway station.'

'I'll have to try, all the same. It doesn't look like stopping for hours and even if it does I don't fancy paddling through six inches of water to the other end of the town.'

'Go ahead, if you must, only I'm warning you that you'll be wasting your time, having just worked through the list myself. Two of them don't answer and the third has a recorded message, saying please try again later. There's a place out on the Dorchester road who might have someone, but it'd take them twenty minutes to get here and they're not all that reliable.'

'Haven't you got your car today?'

'Oh, sure, and I'd be happy to drive you wherever you want to go, only Elfrieda has prior claim. Hers has gone in for servicing and she asked me to lay on a taxi to stand by to take her home, which is how I happen to be so well informed on the current situation.'

'So you'll take her in yours?'

'When she's ready, which could be in ten minutes or two hours. Sorry about that.'

'Oh, it's all right, thank you, Len, but I wish I knew her secret. I can't see anyone waiting around for me for a couple of hours, while I made up my mind whether I was ready to leave or not.'

'Oh, come on! It's not like that at all. She's got someone coming to see her, that's the problem. Business appointment and she can't tell how long it may go on for. Doesn't bother me. I've got hours of work on the script to get through before tomorrow. I can just as easily do it here as at home.'

'Then I'd better follow your noble example,' I said.

53

'Curl up in a corner and learn my lines until the sun come out.'

Hardly was the resolution formed than Kyril came through from the back of the theatre. He did not appear to be hurrying, so it must have been anxiety which made him out of breath and out of humour:

'So here you are, Tessa! I have been waiting for you for such ages. You had forgotten perhaps that you were coming for a drink this evening?'

'Not at all. It was a question of how to get there.'

'But in my car, naturally. We had arranged all that.'

'I don't see any car.'

'How could you? It is out in front. Parking is strictly forbidden here. It is half forbidden on the Esplanade, so I shall be in trouble if you don't hurry up.'

'Okay, I'm all ready. Goodnight, Len. Hope you don't have to wait too long.'

'Surely you must know that I wouldn't desert you,' Kyril said reproachfully, as we crossed the stage and then went down through the auditorium towards the foyer.

'The suspicion was rearing its ugly head,' I replied.

'You should know me better than that. I have been waiting in the foyer for at least twenty minutes.'

I had no intention of arguing with him, although in fact this was the first place I had looked in myself, and had spent almost ten minutes there, before concluding that I had made a mistake and that he was waiting for me by the stage entrance. It would have been tactless to mention this, since clearly his old world code of chivalry prevented his admitting that he had temporarily forgotten all about our appointment, only remembering it again when he was half way home.

EIGHT

It was Len who found her and, according to the medical reckoning, she had then been dead for not less than half an hour. However, this was not so precise an estimate as it sounded because there was no way of establishing whether she had died instantly or remained alive, though unconscious, for some time after the accident. The events which led up to the discovery were as follows:

Soon after Kyril and I left the rain eased off, the sun came out and two minutes later Jamie set off to slosh his way back to his cliff top. Others soon followed his example and by half past six almost the only people left in the theatre were Marples, the stage door keeper, who had just come on duty, Elfrieda, alone in her office, Len at work on his script in the Green Room and Viola. She was the only member of our team who was also appearing in that evening's production, which happened, rather appropriately, to be *Heartbreak House*. The change in the weather had come too late for her and she had realised that she would scarcely be able to get to her car and drive to the cottage before it was time to turn round and come back again. So she had gone to her room to read a book until it was time to dress.

At ten minutes past seven a Mr Roger Padmore had

telephoned the stage door to enquire whether Miss Henshaw was still in the building. Marples was distinctly puzzled by this since it was well known to everyone in Elfrieda's circle that she had her own private telephone line up in the dome. The number was unlisted however and, concluding that Mr Padmore had forgotten it, Marples duly spelt it out for him, only to be told with a trace of impatience that he had been trying to ring it for the last twenty minutes and could get no answer. Would Marples be so good, therefore, as to find out whether she was in some other part of the theatre and, if possible, bring her to the telephone. Presumably not much fancying this errand, Marples replied that it was against the rules for him to leave his post at that hour of the evening and that he would transfer the call to the Green Room.

'All I can tell you,' Len said, when this had been done, 'is that she had a business appointment at six-thirty, so presumably it's still going on and nothing is allowed to interrupt it.'

'I regard that as the most unlikely explanation of all,' Mr Padmore informed him.

'All the same, it has been known. Most people wouldn't have the strength of mind to leave the telephone ringing, but Miss Henshaw is different.'

'I am quite aware of that, but it doesn't account for her not answering it on this occasion.'

'Why not?'

'For the excellent reason that her appointment at six-thirty was with me.'

'Oh . . . Oh, I get it. You want me to let her know you can't make it? You've been held up or something?'

'No, I have not been held up or something. What I should like you to do, if you would be so very good, is to find Miss Henshaw as quickly as you are able and tell her that I have been waiting at her house for three quarters of an hour and that I should be obliged if she would let me know whether she intends to keep our appointment or not.'

'Oh, sure, but listen, I can tell you straight off what the answer will be. You've got it wrong. Miss Henshaw was expecting you to come here, to the theatre.'

There was a long, audible sigh and then Mr Padmore began again:

'That may be your impression and I confess it was also mine until three o'clock this afternoon. When I returned to my office after lunch there was a message from my secretary telling me that Miss Henshaw wished me to call at her home this evening, instead of at her office as we'd arranged.'

'I do think there's got to be some mistake, though, honestly, I do. I mean . . .'

'My secretary has known Miss Henshaw for nearly thirty years and she is not given to mistakes of that kind, I assure you. However, wouldn't you agree there's only one way to find out? I have wasted rather a lot of time already, so if you would be kind enough to do as I ask?'

'Okay, if you insist, but you'd better hang up and wait for me to call you back on the other phone. About five minutes.'

This proved to be an understatement because, although he almost literally ran into Elfrieda in the space of three, as he panted up the ramp, his promise to Mr Padmore was instantly forgotten in the shock of what he saw.

She was lying about midway between the dome and the ground floor, the wheelchair having tipped over on its side, with the front of it jammed up against the outer wall of a right hand curve. Although he did not dare to go very close, still less touch her, he knew for certain and at once that she was dead.

Hours later, still in a state of partial shock and unable to stop talking, he confided to Viola and myself that his first coherent thought had been that this would mean the end of his job; his second that, in some inexplicable fashion, Melanie had been responsible for this new disaster.

NINE

'Inexplicable is the word,' was Robin's comment. 'And why should he have thought that, I wonder? Had he seen her walking on the cliffs too?'

'I don't think so,' I replied, plunging my fork into the lobster armoricain, 'although he may well have heard rumours that she was back in town. It's more likely, though, that his remark was inspired by the absolute obsession everyone at the Rotunda has about Melanie. One way and another, she managed to set a lot of cats among all those pigeons. Their feathers got so ruffled that, however irrationally, whenever something awful happened the automatic reaction was to blame it on her.'

This was on Saturday, the day after Elfrieda's funeral. The local dignitaries and business contingent had turned out in force for it, which was a lot more than they had ever done for her live productions and, after a good deal of argument, acrimony and vacillation, it had been agreed that as a mark of respect the theatre should remain closed until the following Monday.

As this shut-down applied to rehearsals as well, I had at first been ready to jump at Viola's offer of a lift to London for the weekend, but when I rang Robin to tell him of this plan, he suggested coming to Dearehaven instead, so that we could explore the countryside and maybe go for a spin round the harbour in the *Saucy Sal*.

Since the warm, dry weather had by then returned in double strength and the newspaper headlines were given over to such witticisms as 'Phew!' and 'Britain Scorches', this struck me as a sensible move and when I went over to Dorchester by taxi to meet the London train I was not altogether surprised to see Toby alighting from it as well.

Kind as ever, Viola, then on the point of setting forth for a weekend in London, had insisted that there was plenty of room for all three of us at the cottage. However, after she had gone Toby remarked that it was curious how often large women were so fatally attracted to bijou surroundings and that he remembered Viola's flat in Chiswick being equally claustrophobic. Furthermore, although it was true that he could not actually see the cliff edge, he knew it was there and would not be able to sleep for worrying about it. Knowing what we were up against, Robin and I surrendered at once and booked the whole party into the Green Man. So far, all the indications pointed to the fact that its illustrious reputation had not been over-rated.

'Was she really such a menace?' Robin asked, referring to my remarks about Melanie.

'Hard to say. I only met her once, but she struck me as rather a jolly, extroverted kind of girl. On the make, no doubt, but she'd had it rough all her life, so who can blame her for that? I think her chief crime was in driving a wedge between Elfrieda and the company, breaking up their tight, secure little world. Not deliberately perhaps, but it was happening and they couldn't stand it. It made them feel excluded and unloved and you know what that does to people in our profession.'

'It would be interesting to know where she's gone,' Robin said, 'and what she's up to.'

'Nothing good, I daresay. She didn't turn up at the

funeral, you won't be surprised to hear and, so far as I've heard, no one has seen her around lately. I expect she's heard the news about Elfrieda, realised there was no longer any future for her in Dearehaven and that the time had come to move on.'

Toby glanced up with a puzzled expression: 'Isn't there something missing? Do you feel that too, Robin?'

'No, I can't say I do,' Robin admitted, looking the table over, also with a puzzled expression, which was not surprising, considering what was on it.

'Surely this should be the moment when Tessa informs us that, contrary to all the evidence, Elfrieda's death was due to far more sinister causes than a boring old heart attack?'

'Yes, so it is; and it must be very frustrating for her, but I daresay that even she would find it uphill work, in the circumstances. I understand the poor old lady was known to have a weak heart and that her doctor had warned her on numerous occasions not to go gallivanting up and down that ramp unless she had someone with her. It must be a blow, though, Tessa,' he added in solemn tones. 'Are you sure you can't find some tiny flaw that the others have overlooked, anything at all suspicious or out of place to give you a start?'

'Well, I don't know if you'd call it suspicious, but it was certainly out of place. I refer, of course, to the moustache.'

'Oh, do you? Whose moustache?'

'Who knows whose? It was a false one and it was in the little back bedroom behind her office. When they carried her in there, they found it sitting up on the dressing table. It's hard to believe that Elfrieda had some secret kink about male impersonation. In any case, it would have been quite superfluous, she already looked like a man without any make-up at all.'

'Oh well, yes, I suppose that's better than nothing. But she certainly wasn't killed by a false moustache and I suppose in a place like the Rotunda you'd expect to find articles of that kind lying around just about anywhere.'

'And she did get a bash on the head,' I reminded them, 'and furthermore it was inflicted while she was still alive.'

'So another small ray of hope? But it won't be enough, I'm afraid. Anyone whose wheelchair had overturned and come crashing down on to a concrete floor would be unusually lucky not to sustain a blow on the head and, since death from a heart attack isn't necessarily instantaneous, there is nothing very sinister in the fact that she was still alive, although probably unconscious, when the accident happened.'

'I'm aware of that, Robin, and, as you've said, it is rather a pity. Not because I want to stir up trouble either. God knows, it's going to be hard enough to stagger through the season without any extra complications. Elfrieda was the complete autocrat so far as the administration was concerned and wouldn't delegate a thing, if she could avoid it, so there are going to be endless hurdles and pitfalls ahead.'

'So why be disappointed that you haven't got a murder to cope with as well?'

'Oh, simply from a detached point of view, as of one who had no personal interest at stake. I don't know whether either of you has noticed it, but if there had been something non-accidental about this, it would have been one of those rare cases where every single potential suspect had a perfect opportunity to spend ten or fifteen minutes alone with the victim just before her death. Only think of it! At one end of the spectrum we have Kyril claiming to have been waiting by the foyer entrance between six o'clock and twenty past, although if it's true he must have been wearing a heavy disguise because I certainly didn't see him there. Then there's Jamie. As soon as the rain stopped he went stamping off, ostensibly to walk home, but there's no proof that he actually did so. He need have gone no further than round the corner and back into the foyer. Next comes Viola, who says she spent the entire time in her dressing room, but again there's no proof that she didn't leave it at one point and make a quick trip to the dome. The same thing applies to Len, who was supposed to have been quietly working away, all on his own, in the Green Room.'

Robin was not impressed: 'Quite apart from the fact that none of these people had the vestige of a motive, what you've just told us is almost enough to prove their innocence. I should remind you that the guilty ones invariably go through no end of hoops to provide themselves with an alibi.'

'In that case,' Toby announced, 'Tessa's wish is likely to be granted, after all. I am now convinced that the old party was indeed murdered and, furthermore, I am able to name the culprit.'

If breath was not totally bated, at least we paid him the compliment of laying down our forks.

'The mysterious Padmore,' he told us solemnly. 'I have it all! Obviously, his telephone call was faked.'

'Yes,' I agreed. 'I had come to the same conclusion and really, you know, it would have done very nicely. All he had to do was to arrive ten minutes early for his appointment with Elfrieda, knock her out, release the brake on the wheelchair, give it a good hard push, then nip round to her house and produce his story of there being some mix-up. It's such a simple answer that it almost comes into Robin's category of proven innocence. Except that a child of three could break that sort of alibi in two seconds.'

'Although he did claim that the message altering the appointment came through his secretary,' Robin pointed out, 'so I suppose that might complicate things? Otherwise, you'd have to drag in a bit of collusion.'

'Not necessarily. He told Len that the message had come while he was out at lunch, which means that it would only have been a matter of telephoning this secretary and putting on a funny voice. However, although it's a lovely idea, I'm afraid we have to throw it out. For one thing, he's not the mysterious Padmore, by any stretch of the imagination. He is, or was, Elfrieda's lawyer and no pillar of respectability has ever been straighter. His firm have been looking after the Henshaw family for two generations.'

'Highly suspect,' Toby said, laying siege to his lobster again. 'I expect she'd just found out that he'd been diddling them for two generations as well.'

'Leaving the wretched Padmore out of it for the moment,' Robin said, 'I did notice one rather interesting omission in Tessa's list of suspects.'

'You mean Melanie, of course? I know and it's too bad, isn't it? I'd love to have included her in the game too, but she simply wouldn't fit. The others I've mentioned were already inside the theatre when Elfrieda died, but Melanie wasn't and there's no way she could have got in and out again unnoticed.'

'On the other hand, you did say that Jamie could have walked out by the stage door and then in through the foyer. Why wouldn't the same objection apply to him?'

'Because he was such a familiar feature. All the front of the house staff are so used to seeing him wandering in and out that his presence wouldn't have impinged. He's your actual picture on the wall now, but Melanie was a very different cup of tea. She's always been an object of curiosity and still more so since the rumour started circulating that she was back in Dearehaven. Everyone would have been agog for a sight of her. The only time, so far as I can see, when she might have got in without attracting attention was just before the start of a performance, when there's a terrific crush of people skirmishing around in the foyer and the box office staff are up to their eyes. But it's never like that between six and seven in the evening. That's one of the deadest periods of the whole day.'

At this point I found that I had lost their attention because someone at the next table to ours had ordered crêpes suzettes and there can be few more engrossing pastimes than watching them being put together by a deft and accomplished hand. However, for once my mind wasn't really on it, because the moment I saw the waiter wheeling his trolley load of ingredients and utensils over to the table I was gripped by a new and strange idea. Mulling it over, as he expertly tilted his pan this way and that, set it over the flame, then coyly withdrew it again, I realised that, after all, I could add Melanie to my hypothetical list of suspects in the non-existent murder case.

However, I was not yet ready to pass on the news to anyone else and, when the pancake pantomime was over and conversation resumed, it was confined exclusively to discussing plans for the afternoon.

TEN

Robin was obliged to go back to London on Sunday evening, but Toby elected to stay on for another week. Dearehaven appealed to him, as I had guessed it would, for he has a great affection for spas and watering places with a genteel, Edwardian flavour about them. However, in answer to my enquiry as to whether he would be able to keep his room at the Green Man, he told me that he did not intend to ask for it. The temptation to keep popping into the dining room would prove too strong, undoubtedly reducing his life expectation by a good ten years, and he had therefore booked himself into the Royal Metropolitan Hotel.

This was a vast, granite coloured building, dominating the Esplanade and looking as though it had been built as a prison during the Napoleonic wars, but it suited Toby to perfection because his bathroom alone was the size of a billiard room. His single complaint was that, although the Palm Court still existed, there was no longer a three-piece orchestra to go with it, but since he appeared to be the only guest in residence this was probably understandable.

We did not see much of each other during the first few days because I was back at work and he would not come to Viola's in the evening, for fear of running into Jamie, to whom he was absolutely devoted but never wanted to see. He still refused to put his life at risk by dining at the Green Man and on the single occasion when he had enticed me into the Grill Room of the Royal Metropolitan, which conformed in scale and spirit to St Pancras Station, although the food was unexpectedly good and the wine exceptionally so, I found the heavy, muted atmosphere so overpowering as to destroy the appetite.

So with a view to breaking out of this impasse, I suggested that on Saturday we should go for a picnic. I had been prepared for a stream of opposition to this proposal, which is exactly what I got.

He began by asking whether, since neither of us had a car, I was planning to spread out the cloth in a bus shelter.

'Not at all,' I replied. 'Some quiet spot on the beach is what I had in mind.'

'Are you raving? In case you haven't taken a look at the beach recently, allow me to tell you that at no time during the daylight hours is it occupied by less than three quarters of a million people.'

'Not that beach, I was thinking of one a bit further along. It's called Rocky Cove and it's at the bottom of Viola's cliff.'

'In that case, you have doubtless arranged for a helicopter to take us down there?'

'No, that won't be necessary. You see, Jamie arrived at Viola's yesterday before she got home, so I was able to consult him in depth and this cove is not nearly so inaccessible as you'd imagine. All you have to do is walk downhill towards the town for about a hundred yards and you're practically on sea level. Then you walk back along the beach again and there you are!'

'With five hundred other people?'

'Wrong! They avoid it like the plague and there are reasons. There's no sand for the children to play on and no one can swim there either because it's a carpet of rocks. Even at high tide they're only about two feet below the surface and most of them are covered with black, slimy seaweed. Also the cliff is rapidly eroding and there's a sign up to warn people about falling rocks, but the best bit of all is that if we time it right we shall be cut off.'

'Cut off from what?'

'Intruders. That's another deterrent. When the tide's up, the only way out of the cove is through knee-high water; the same, as you will be quick to see, applying to the only way in.'

'And what happens to us? Do we sit on a crumbling ledge, watching the water lapping round our ankles?'

'No, we shall be quite safe and comfortable. I've checked it out very thoroughly with Jamie. The only time the beach gets covered right over is once a year, on 22nd March, I think he said, or it may have been the 23rd. What we have to do is to arrive when the tide is coming in and stay until it has started to go out again. On Saturday, our E.T.A. should be between midday and one o'clock, so what could be more convenient?'

'It sounds quite practical,' Toby admitted, 'but I do wish your informant had been anyone but Jamie. Can we trust him?'

'Yes, we can. I know he's capable of contemplating your death by drowning with a detachment bordering on indifference, but that doesn't apply to mine. We're now in the second week of rehearsals and he has enough problems on his hands without having to replace me in the cast.'

This appeared to satisfy him and it was arranged that he would come by taxi to Viola's cottage, where I should be standing by at twelve hundred hours with the rugs and picnic basket. However, before all this came to pass, there had been a minor, though, in its way, momentous development at the Rotunda.

Naturally everyone who knew her, either personally or by reputation, had been bursting with curiosity about the disposal of Elfrieda's property, most particularly the Rotunda Theatre, of which she had been sole owner. The only information to have come our way by the time Toby and I were laying our plans for the picnic was that there were two executors to the will, of whom Roger Padmore was one and a cousin named Douglas Henshaw, whom none of us had ever set eyes on, the other.

Obviously, the day-to-day running of the theatre could not have been left to take care of itself, so a small *ad hoc* committee had been formed for this purpose, with Mr Padmore in the chair. The other members were the two resident directors, the Company and Front of House managers and James Crowther. The co-executor was unable to take any part, having recently broken his ankle during a game of golf.

The first meeting had been convened on Friday morning, when the Chairman had taken the opportunity to inform the rest of them about the terms of the will. By lunch time the news, or some part of it, was known to everyone in the building and on the same evening Viola and I got the full details when Jamie arrived for his six o'clock session with the champagne and tapestry.

He began by explaining that the will had not been substantially altered since the death of Elfrieda's father, when she had inherited the bulk of his vast fortune. One or two of the beneficiaries had died in the interval and various codicils had been added over the years, one of them very recently, but in essence it remained the same.

'And what it boils down to is this,' he said. 'After bequests to the domestic staff, plus minor sums to one or two relatives and godchildren, the residue all goes to Cousin Douglas with the broken ankle.'

'And what did Douglas do to deserve such bounty?' Viola asked. 'She never mentioned him to me; I didn't even know of his existence until the other day.'

'Nor I, but Padmore gave me the story in dry tones over a dry sherry at the Royal Metropolitan. I saw Toby in the bar, by the way, Tessa. Looking rather wan, I thought. Is he all right?'

'Hard work takes its toll,' I reminded him.

'Could we leave Toby out of this for a moment,' Viola asked, 'and get back to Douglas?'

'Yes, and there is a moral, you'll be pleased to hear.'

'The moral being?'

'That you cannot cast your bread too widely or pre-maturely upon the waters.'

Viola did indeed look rather pleased to hear this, as well she might, and proceeded at once to put precept into practice by refilling his glass.

'How kind of you, darling! Well now, it appears that Douglas was very attentive to Elfrieda at one point. Not in her youth because she was years older than him, but during her lonely, arid middle age, when it obviously made a memorable impression. He was what they used to describe as a young blade, just down from university and starting in the family firm; one of them, at any rate. Hand-some, according to Padmore, and very much in demand by all the young blade-esses. But either because he saw it as a solid investment or because he genuinely found her companionable, he devoted a lot of time to Elfrieda. They used to go for long tramps together and he took her to plays and concerts as far away as Bristol, would you believe? It must have been an intoxicating thrill in that bleak existence. It all came to an end after the war, when Douglas married and built himself a love nest in the country, but it was obviously an idyllic period for Elfrieda and, as we now see, she never ceased to be grateful.'

'And his attachment could have been genuine,' I remarked. 'Quite a lot of young men enjoy the company of older women with brains and taste and, if he had simply been grinding an axe, surely he would have kept it up to some extent after his marriage and made sure that his wife did too?'

'I expect you're right,' Viola said, concealing her impatience with some difficulty, 'but I'd like to point out that just now his motives are somewhat immaterial.'

'Except that, since he is now presumably the sole owner of those boards we tread upon, it might be useful to know whether he is honest Joe, or a greedy grabber. And it might tell us something interesting about Elfrieda.'

'What would that be?' Jamie asked, apparently more ready than Viola was to be diverted by irrelevancies, but once again she interrupted.

'How could that possibly matter, now she's dead? I do wish you'd allow Jamie to get on with it. Is it true, Jamie? Does this Douglas now own the Rotunda?'

'He does at this precise moment, but I doubt if he will do so for long. In fact, in the cautious view of Roger Padmore, he won't have much choice. By the time the death duties and legacies have been paid, the Rotunda may be about the only thing left, apart from a few cottages on long lease to exceptionally healthy tenants.'

There was a moment or two of shocked silence and then Viola, speaking for us both on this occasion, said:

'My dear, I don't understand what you mean. I was under the impression that Elfrieda was absolutely loaded, that she owned about half of Dearehaven, for a start?'

'So she did, dearest, once upon a time in the long, long ago. She's been selling it off, bit by bit, for years and using the money to shore up her precious old theatre. Right against Padmore's advice, needless to say, but we all know what a big difference that would have made.'

'But doesn't the theatre make a profit?'

'I've always heard that it did,' I admitted.

'So have we all, I daresay, but we've been rather blind, you know. We might have known that, with those stylish productions and expensive casts in a theatre seating three hundred, you'd need to charge at least five pounds a head to have any chance of breaking even; and if you did that in Dearehaven you'd play to empty houses.'

'Yes, I know, but wasn't the difference made up by grants and so on? What about all those brewers and people, who were sponsoring her?'

'The answer is that they bought their prestige rather cheaply. It might have covered most of the expenses fifteen years ago, but not any more, and if there was one quality Elfrieda lacked it was the ability to beg. The Rotunda has been losing money consistently for years and instead of taking the hat round or cutting down on expenses, she simply sold off another row of houses to make up the deficit. There was a certain mad grandeur about it, which one cannot but admire.'

'That's all very fine,' Viola protested, 'but she must have known that it couldn't go on for ever.'

'It didn't have to, did it, darling? She was over seventy, in great pain most of the time and her heart was rapidly giving out. The big surprise must have been to wake up in the morning and find she was still alive.'

'And she didn't give a damn what happened when she ceased to be?'

'My dear girl, aren't you being unfair? Why should she

have given a damn? The only happiness and satisfaction she got from her life didn't begin until she was almost sixty. During her last decade she gave a great deal of pleasure to a great many people and provided work for a great many more. Some of them made their reputations here, myself included. In my opinion, Elfrieda has paid her debt to posterity with compound interest.'

He did not add, as he might have, that Viola also had cause for gratitude, and I asked him what sort of future there would be for the Rotunda now.

'Rather a bleak one, I'm sorry to say. Presumably, we shall stagger on until October. It would really be a false economy to close down earlier, with so many people under contract for the full season. After that, who can say? Padmore thinks it's likely that Douglas will cut his losses and get what he can for it. It won't be much because Elfrieda managed to get a preservation order slapped on it, so it can't be pulled down to make way for office blocks. Disappointing for him because half an acre on that site is the kind of thing property developers dream about.'

Viola said: 'So poor old Douglas only got rather a shabby reward, after all.'

'Yes, and the most sickening part of all must be to know that if only Elfrieda had had the courtesy to postpone her death for another day or two, the reward would have been just that much more worthwhile.'

I had a flash of inspiration concerning the meaning behind this remark, though was glad Viola was there to get it in straight terms:

'Why, Jamie? What difference would that have made?'

'One can't be certain, of course,' he replied, 'and Padmore told me this in strictest confidence, so keep it under your hats; but you remember he had an appointment with her on the evening of her death?'

'Which wasn't kept,' I reminded them. 'There was some mix-up.'

'Exactly! I suppose the poor old thing had been feeling groggy all day and became confused. Anyway, the point is that in Padmore's opinion the purpose of the meeting was to instruct him to revoke her most recent codicil. He had urged her to do so and she'd told him that she would think it over and let him have her answer in a day or two. It concerned a little matter of ten thousand pounds.'

'Who'd she left that to?'

'You mean you can't guess?'

'Oh, no! Not Melanie?'

'Who else? It was to pay her expenses for a drama school course, plus board and lodging.'

'And the clause still stands? She'll get the money?'

'Every last penny,' he replied with great conviction.

'Which makes it still more frustrating that this is not a murder case,' I told Toby, as we spread our rug and table-cloth over the flattest expanse of rock we had been able to find, 'for now we have the classic motive. Not many people would sneeze at ten thousand pounds and it must have been beyond the wildest dreams of someone like Melanie.'

'Provided she knew she was to get it.'

'Oh, I expect she did. I am sure Elfrieda would have used it as a veiled bribe, to encourage her to be a good girl and stay with poor old adopted Auntie. The car and driving lessons indicate that she wasn't above such devices.'

'You can't say they proved very successful, however.'

'Probably because she had no conception of the breed of viper she was nursing in her bosom. If this really had been murder, I should start from the premise that Melanie couldn't wait to get her hands on all that money, couldn't tolerate the prospect of being a good girl, possibly for years and always with the threat that Elfrieda might change her mind and all the goodness be wasted. So she decided it would be safer if poor old Auntie dropped off the hook right away, but first of all she had to stage a disappearing act, so that whatever happened no blame could be attached to her. It's such a nice theory, because it explains why, with everything to lose, as it then seemed, she should have walked out. With ten thousand pounds in the bank, she could have afforded a brand new car and driving lessons for half the female population of Dearehaven.'

'I do feel for you,' Toby said, 'but it is not such a great catastrophe. You may have lighted on the perfect culprit with the perfect motive, but don't forget that you were the first to point out that it would have been impossible for Melanie to have got in and out of the building unobserved.'

'Unfortunately, I may have been a little hasty there. I have since thought of a method whereby she could have overcome even that obstacle.'

'Oh, that is bad news! Do tell me, though, how could she have done it? Black wig, sunglasses, all that caper?'

'No, none of that would have got her past the main entrance, if she'd rolled up between six and seven in the evening, which was the original assumption. Wandering about the theatre in that sort of amateurish disguise would only have succeeded in drawing attention to herself and would also have indicated that she was up to no good. So long as she retained her own identity, in the last resort she could always claim that her purpose was entirely innocent; in other words, that the lamb had repented and was attempting to re-enter the flock. But, thinking it over, and with a little help from the waiter and his trolley at the Green Man, I hit on one splendidly ingenious method she could have used.'

'How very clever of you! And clever of her too, I suppose, seeing that she must have thought of it first? We must at least give her equal credit.'

'Not quite equal, because up to a point it was a well rehearsed routine. She had used and succeeded with it before. It was simply a matter of adapting it to the new circumstances.'

'Do explain!'

'You remember my telling you that the only time she could have slipped in unnoticed was about ten minutes before the last bell, when three quarters of the audience was still jostling around in the foyer and things were at their most hectic for the staff?'

'I do, indeed. A good point, in my opinion.'

'So what was to prevent her doing exactly that? Oh, not on Tuesday, when Elfrieda died, of course not, but on Monday, approximately twenty-two hours in advance of the event?'

Toby looked disappointed: 'Oh, surely not? Twenty-two hours would have meant such a tedious wait. And where could she have hidden herself all the time? I do remember the story of her spending the night in a laundry basket, but that only lasted until the following morning.'

'But this time she'd have known her way around and also what everyone in the building would have been doing at a given moment. She could have holed up indefinitely, mainly by using two separate bases which were connected with each other in such a way that she would have been able to pass from one to the other without the faintest risk of being seen.'

'My dear Tessa, you fascinate me! This is so much more riveting than I was prepared for and I begin to feel as sorry as you that, since there has not been a murder, we are only skipping through the realms of fantasy.'

'Nevertheless, you'd be interested to hear how she could have brought it off, if it had been murder?'

'Intensely,' he admitted, spreading a lump of pâté on to his wheaty crisp.

'Then listen carefully. When Melanie enters the theatre on Monday evening at approximately ten minutes to eight, she threads her way discreetly through the thick crowd to the far side of the foyer and the door leading to the ramp. She knows that Elfrieda will have already left, so there will be no human traffic on the ramp and also that the office will be empty, and so this is her destination.'

At this point I felt compelled to break off the reconstruction because the pâté was disappearing rather rapidly and I had some catching up to do.

Resuming a minute or so later, I said: 'I don't know whether it was locked, but in any case Melanie would have armed herself with a key and, once inside, she was not only safe for the night, but had a comfortable bed to spend it on.'

'Quite so. And come the dawn?'

'In my version, she allows herself a clear margin of half an hour or so before Elfrieda's regular arrival time and then, around nine-thirty, descends to her second hiding place and camps out in the bar.'

'You don't say! Would she have had a key to the bar as well?'

'Why not? A resourceful girl like that! And no risk of running into one of the cleaners on the way. She travels by service lift.'

'Oh, of course she does. How stupid of me not to have guessed it! Tell me, though: she's quite sturdy, I understand? Would there have been room for her?'

'Masses. I took a good look at it at lunch yesterday and it's a great solid and spacious Victorian contraption, specially built, I daresay, to carry all those heavy tomes and museum exhibits. No problem there.'

'How very satisfactory! And could she have spent the whole day in the bar?'

'Why not, since there's no matinée on Tuesday? She'd have been perfectly safe until the ladies came on duty at seven, which in any case was long past zero hour.'

'The moment when, having sailed skywards again, she comes bursting out of the dumb waiter, causing the old lady to suffer a heart attack, which I must say I regard as highly plausible. My own reaction would have been almost identical.'

'Although I admit to being a bit in the dark on details. For instance, did Melanie, assuming Elfrieda to be already dead, push the wheelchair down the ramp, so as to give verisimilitude to a straightforward heart attack? Or did Elfrieda, confronted by that terrifying apparition, guess what was in store and make a frantic attempt to escape? One thing I can tell you, though; if this were fact instead of fantasy, it would have tidied up one other loose end, which still hangs by an uncounted thread.'

'Which is that?'

'The message to Mr Padmore's secretary, purporting to come from Elfrieda, to change the appointment, but which Elfrieda appears to have had no knowledge of, since she had asked Len to hang around indefinitely, so as to drive her home afterwards.'

'And you see Melanie's hand in that too? Or her voice, rather?'

'Yes, I do. Don't forget that I've given her a whole night on her own, up in the dome. If for no other reason than to alleviate the boredom, she would undoubtedly have had a good snoop through Elfrieda's desk, including her engagement diary. In fact, one could say that it would have been essential to find out as much as she could about the following day's programme.'

'And so came across the item concerning this appointment?'

'Which would have been bad news; specially if she'd also seen a note about the car going in for service. She'd have realised at once that there was a strong chance that Elfrieda and Mr Padmore would leave together, so that he could give her a lift home. My theory is that she waited until it was fairly certain that he would be out to lunch, then used the bar telephone to call his secretary, imitating Elfrieda's voice. In fact, you know, Toby, it's that incident of the false telephone message which really started me off on all this. No one has made any attempt to account for it.'

'Yes, I'm sure you're right, but I must caution you against bleating about it to anyone else. It could make you unpopular.'

'I've no intention of it,' I assured him. 'I've only told you to show you what a good case could be made, if one has a mind to, but that's the end of it. The poor old Rotunda is in a precarious enough state already, without my adding to the problem.'

'By the way, you haven't told me how Melanie could have managed to get out of the building, but I suppose it would be too much to hope that you haven't thought of that?'

'Yes, and I can't see that it would have been at all difficult. She had only to stay hidden upstairs until after the second interval, when the bar closed and the house-lights were down, go back to the ground floor, walk two yards to the emergency exit and vanish into the night.'

'There now, so you have not overlooked a single detail, and perhaps, after all, it won't be wasted. Melanie will have to surface, you know, sooner or later, if she is to claim her legacy and then perhaps they will start asking some of the questions to which you will have all the answers.'

'I doubt it, Toby. If she's as bright as I take her to be, she'll lie low for a few weeks, but keeping constantly on the move, so that no one could expect her to produce a solid alibi for any given day. I don't imagine the penalties for ducking out and breaking the probation rules will be very tough, specially now that she's a girl of means and specially, also, if she has managed to keep out of trouble in the meantime.'

However, keeping out of trouble was the one thing that Melanie had not managed to do, as we discovered only half an hour later. The tide had just turned on the start of its inward journey and Toby proposed that, while there was still time, we should work off our lunch by taking a stroll round to the bay beyond, the seaweed, as he pointed out, always being greener on the other side. Although, true to Jamie's prediction, we had not seen another soul, we nevertheless felt dubious about leaving Viola's rugs and picnic basket unguarded in the middle of the beach. So, rather than lug them with us or take it in turns to go for a walk, we compromised by packing everything up, with the intention of concealing it behind a large pile of loose rocks at the edge of the cliff.

'I wonder if this is wise, though?' Toby said, as we approached it. 'They are ominously new looking. Perhaps the cliff is eroding so rapidly that we shall return to find all our belongings buried under a new fall.'

That would not have been half so bad, however, as the discovery of what had been buried under the last one, for he had hardly uttered this gloomy prediction than we both stopped dead in our tracks. Sticking out from under the white mound was a plump and youthful female hand, with a few inches of arm above it, showing the frill of a scarlet sleeve.

Jamie had been quite wrong in one respect and, whatever else might happen, Melanie would never be able to claim her ten thousand pounds.

ELEVEN

Toby tossed a coin. I couldn't swear that he cheated, but I expect he did, because he thrust it rather hastily back into his pocket, and I was the one to be left behind to stand guard, while he walked back to Viola's house to telephone the police.

'Well, why don't we both go?' he asked, interrupting my stream of complaints about this unfair division of labour. 'She is not likely to run away this time.'

I reminded him that not even Jamie was infallible and of how dreadful it would be if some party of laughing, innocent children should take it into their heads to explore the cove, and also that, if the local police were as dim as some people had implied, it might take them hours to locate the exact spot on their own.

When he had gone I spread out my rug again and settled down to wait, and the wait seemed endless. I had no cigarettes, nothing to read and nothing whatever to do except re-live the recent gruesome experience and count the minutes until my release came.

After a whole miserable hour of it, it dawned on me that the tide was rapidly encroaching and that before long I should be forced to remove myself to a point higher up the beach. One thing I was certain of, though; in no circumstances did I intend to remain there until the moment came when I should have to paddle my way out; still less to remain nobly at my post, surrounded by water on three sides and a dead girl on the fourth.

This resolve gave rise to speculations as to what would occur if the rescue team did indeed arrive too late. Presumably, Melanie would have to remain where she was until the tide receded again, for it was hard to see how she could be removed through waist-high water over those jagged slippery rocks. This, of course, must be all to the good, so far as one member of the human race was concerned, since, on the assumption that her death was due neither to suicide nor accident, it followed that the murderer's motive in choosing this remote spot had been to put as much time as possible between the deed and its discovery. In fact, it was bad luck for him that the time had been so relatively short. But for a fluke, weeks could have elapsed before she was found.

However, this line of reasoning did not produce any big thrills because I was now more than half convinced that the imaginary reconstruction I had just given Toby was quite as nonsensical as I had pretended and furthermore that the two deaths were quite unconnected. It was far more likely, I now realised, that the doctor's verdict on Elfrieda had been correct and that Melanie had suffered the fate which was liable to befall any girl unwise enough to have put herself in the position of having no fixed address, while carrying around a large sum of cash. In all likelihood, she had been murdered by the young man Jamie had seen her out with on that Monday evening. No one had seen her afterwards, whereas, at that time, Elfrieda still had twenty-four hours of life left to her.

I was nearly convinced that this must be the answer, and yet there was still room for one small, obstinate doubt. There was no accounting for it, but in some unidentifiable fashion it was associated in my mind with that single brief and horrifying sight of the plump, innocent looking hand, sticking out from under the pile of rocks. It had carried a message of some sort and I wished that I had the courage to return and look at it again. I was still endeavouring, somewhat half-heartedly, to summon it when my vigil was brought to an end by the arrival of a uniformed out-rider from the Dearehaven Police Force. He was followed a second or two later by two more men carrying a folded stretcher, with three slower movers, hampered by their heavy gear, bringing up the rear. I folded my rug once more and walked over to greet them.

The eldest of the party, a red-faced, middle-aged man in plain clothes, detached himself from the others and asked me if I would be Miss Crichton. I assured him that I would and made a wide, sweeping gesture with my left arm at the lumps of fallen cliff, where his business lay. In doing so, it instantly came to me exactly what there had been about that lifeless hand which had started the doubts and questions in the recesses of my mind.

The red-faced man then introduced himself as Detective Inspector Watson, asked for and noted down various particulars and announced that he would be calling on me later for a full statement. Permission to leave then having been granted, I stumbled over the rocks, along the neighbouring stretch of beach and up the path to Viola's house.

Toby and Jamie were seated on the terrace, drinking champagne and orange juice and looking as though they hadn't a care in the world. I daresay they hadn't, but the sight of the festive little scene inflamed my sense of martyrdom almost to the point of paranoia. However, Toby explained that the delay in despatching the rescue team had been no fault of his. Laden down as he was, it had been necessary to stagger all the way to Jamie's house, to use his telephone, Viola having gone off to do her matinée, very thoughtlessly omitting to leave the key under the mat.

I caught a whiff of sarcasm here, since he was doubtless aware that I had a front door key in my bag and had very thoughtlessly forgotten all about Viola's matinée. Jamie naturally possessed keys to every part of the cottage and he could also be very diplomatic when it suited him. He poured oil on the troubled waters by presenting me with a glass of the lovely iced mixture, before proceeding to question me in the most sympathetic manner imaginable on my recent ordeal. There was probably some guile in this too, and he was hoping that I would reveal some unusual and piquant touch which might come in handy for a plot, but I found myself becoming expansive under all this kind attention, anxious indeed to repay him in his favourite coin and I said:

'As a matter of fact, there was one rather curious and puzzling feature. I hardly noticed it at the time and the significance only struck me after the police arrived. I didn't mention it to them, there didn't seem any point, but maybe you'll agree that it could be important. You remember how Melanie used to. . . ?'

As I reached this crucial point, Viola came prancing out on to the terrace and cut me off in mid-flow. My chance did not come again either, because when she had sat goggle-eyed through Toby's recital of how our picnic had ended, had asked all the predictable questions and made all the predictable comments, the conversation turned to other matters because she too had news to impart. The pleasure of our company was requested on the following day for luncheon at the home of Sir Douglas and Lady Henshaw. The invitation had come via Roger Padmore, who had explained that, since Douglas was still immobilised by his broken ankle and unable to visit his new property and employees, he was hoping at least to meet some of these under his own roof.

'Including you, Toby, of course,' Viola assured him. 'I gather that as soon as he heard you were here, he was mad keen to meet you.'

'I shall certainly go,' Jamie said. 'I think the time has now come when we should all start being very nice to Douglas.'

'It has not come for me, though,' Toby informed them. 'Nor does he have to meet me under his own or anyone else's roof. Besides, I hate parties and I've had more than enough excitement for one week. I intend to go home tomorrow, to recuperate from my holiday.'

This might have been my cue for reintroducing the topic of Melanie, but no one else seemed inclined to do so and on reflection I decided to save my special bit of news for Robin's telephone call, which fortunately came through as usual, at about seven o'clock.

'It was her left hand, you see,' I told him, having described the afternoon's events yet again.

'What was so sensational about it?'

'Lack of adornment, mainly. Just one ring and it looked quite expensive. The only time I got a close-up view of her in life was on that one occasion in Elfrieda's office and she was wearing at least two to each finger. Awful cheap, trashy looking things they were too, so no one could possibly have been tempted to steal them.'

'So presumably all but one dropped off when she fell?'

'If she fell; and I don't see why they should have. Don't you agree it's more likely that she may have removed them herself, in order to replace them with one which was not cheap or trashy at all, like, let's say, an engagement ring?'

86

'I suppose it's possible. Was she going around with any-one in particular?'

'Not that I know of, but if she was it would clear up one or two mysteries. That confusion about her stealing the petty cash, for instance, and Elfrieda insisting that she hadn't. In other words, Melanie didn't run away because she was a thief, she ran away to get married, knowing that if Elfrieda got wind of it she'd put all sorts of obstacles in the way. Then I suppose it struck her that she'd have nothing to lose by bringing the young man to Dearehaven and trying to work her way back into Elfrieda's favour. It might have come off too; the old tartar obviously had a romantic streak under that harsh exterior.'

'Yes, you could be right, but surely it's all rather irrele-vant now? Since both poor ladies are no longer with us ... ?'

'But, Robin, can't you see, that's the whole point? It raises an entirely new set of questions. Elfrieda's death may well have been due to natural causes, I'm not dis-puting that any more, but Melanie's most certainly was not; or accident either.'

'Why not? She could have fallen over the cliff in the dark, or been lying underneath when part of it collapsed.'

'Highly improbable. Why would she have been walking about all alone up there in the dark? Or lying all alone on that rather uninviting beach, for that matter? She wasn't wearing a bathing suit. I happen to know that because part of her dress was showing.'

'So the idea is that she was killed, most likely by the young man she was seen with, whom she may or may not have been intending to marry?'

'Possibly, but so much depends on when it happened. It needn't necessarily have been on the same evening that Jamie saw her. That was almost two weeks ago, so there's a hell of a long gap.'

87

'On the other hand, no one appears to have seen her since then?'

'No, and if we assume that's when it did happen it opens up still wider fields for speculation.'

'Why?'

'Because Elfrieda was still alive by that time and therefore Melanie was still a threat. Jamie never came face to face with this young man. He described him as being fair haired and wearing jeans, which could apply to thousands of people. It needn't necessarily have been a man at all and, although it was hard to dredge up a motive for murdering Elfrieda, this is a very different cup of tea. I could name at least half a dozen highly respected citizens who wanted Melanie out of the way, specially if they thought they'd seen the last of her and then discovered that she'd come tripping back and all the trouble was about to be stirred up again.'

TWELVE

Douglas Henshaw had been knighted some years previously for his services to some political party or other, so they told me, and he and his wife lived in distinctly opulent style in a valley about ten miles inland from Dearehaven, near a village called Hawkham. The house was two-storeyed, red brick and over-gabled and dated from the fifties. It was called Dene Cottage, which was an inverted snobbery if ever I heard one, since it must have contained at least twelve rooms and the grounds included a meadow, copse and stream, not to mention a large cultivated area, complete with swimming pool and greenhouses.

'There had been a cottage of that name here for centuries when I bought the land,' Douglas explained. 'Fallen into rack and ruin, unfortunately, so we had to pull it down and start again, but one hates to see the old names getting lost. Don't you agree?'

In view of what I had heard of his past and also taking into account the approximate age of his son, Charlie, who was down from London for the weekend with his fiancée, I knew that Douglas must be over fifty, but he looked much younger than this, a clean shaven, sleek looking man, with bold and knowing eyes and not a grey hair or an ounce of overweight. He was handsome too and patently conscious of the fact, as different from his cousin Elfrieda as it was possible to imagine.

His right leg was stretched out in front of him and supported by a footstool, and a pair of crutches rested against his armchair. Pointing to them, he apologised for not rising to greet us, explaining that he was supposed to rest his damaged ankle whenever possible.

'Charlie will deputise for me,' he said, directing a fond and complacent smile at his son. 'Find out what the ladies and gentlemen would like to drink, Charlie! Champagne for you, Crowther, I have it on good authority?'

'Most kind!' Jamie murmured, although perhaps he should have been thanking Viola for her good authority.

'Me too,' I said, accepting Douglas's invitation to sit in the chair nearest to his. 'It is such an easy habit to acquire, I'm afraid.'

'Don't be afraid, it's an excellent one. Much better for you than all those mixtures. My wife used to drink pints of it when Charlie was on the way.'

'And he's certainly a good advertisement,' I admitted, truthfully as it happened, for he was an exceptionally good looking young man, with the easy manner which he had inherited or copied from his father. Unlike him, however, he had very blond hair and a deeply discontented expression. There was a suggestion of dissoluteness about him, which I had noticed before in boys who had been doted on and spoilt by their parents.

Douglas reached out and patted my hand: 'How nice of you to say so, Theresa! I suppose I may call you Theresa?'

'If you wish, but I should warn you there's a catch. I don't always respond because I'm mostly called Tessa. Do some people call you Dougie?'

'No, never. At least, not twice.'

'You're lucky not to be in plaster. I was encased in it for three weeks when I broke my ankle and I nearly went out of my mind.'

'Which is precisely why I put my foot down if you'll forgive the pun. My doctor was all for meting out the same punishment, but it's not a serious fracture and in the end we compromised. I'm allowed to keep it strapped up like this, on condition that I don't use it until he comes again next week.'

'All the same, it must be a bore for you?'

'Not at all, it suits me perfectly. In fact, I'm rather hoping that when he comes he will recommend that the treatment should continue indefinitely. I'm bone idle, do you see, and it lets me off all the things I prefer not to do. What is even better is that lovely people like you feel sorry for me and come and sit here and chat me up. I do hope you like confidence tricksters?'

Doing my best to match this somewhat archly flirtatious act, I assumed the Edwardian comedy voice to say:

'Now that you've made me a party to your deceit, I feel I should pay you out by joining the others and leaving you to repent.'

'Then I should pick up my crutches and come hobbling after you. I'm not a slave to my doctor, only to my own indulgences, so I can't lose.'

'No, you don't strike me as a loser,' I admitted.

He beamed delightedly at this, but was prevented from prolonging this rather trying conversation by the fact that two women had now entered the room and my turn had come to be introduced to them. The elder of the pair was Lady Henshaw and the younger Charlie's fiancée, and neither of them looked like losers either. Another interesting resemblance was that they were both noticeably overweight and, as though to announce that this was only a temporary misfortune, both wore clothes a size too small for them.

Lady Henshaw, whose name was Kitty, was a blonde, hard-faced woman, immaculately turned out in a cherry coloured shirt and black patent leather shoes, who looked as though she would have been more at home managing a boutique in Guildford. Whereas Charlie's betrothed had gone to the opposite sartorial extreme and was bursting out of very tight and scruffy looking jeans and a skimpy, sleeveless T-shirt with a heavily scooped out neckline. Her name was Marcia Atterbury and she was an overblown girl in more ways than one, having huge, staring, saucer like eyes, which hardly seemed to blink, a noisy laugh and large teeth, which she frequently bared in a somewhat vulpine smile. However, she may have signalled some special message for the gentlemen, because I noticed that within two minutes Jamie and Len were both at her side, gazing at her like a pair of mesmerised rabbits confronted by a goggle-eyed stoat. However, in Jamie's case, this may have been just part of the policy of being nice to Douglas, which was now extended to take in dependants and future dependants as well.

Their interest naturally caused Charlie to lose his in whatever it was that Viola had been telling him and, considerate as ever, she immediately let him off the hook by saying that she could not wait to ask his mother where she had found those marvellous tulips. Since the marvellous tulips were about as hideous as it was possible for flowers to be, dirty mauve petals and huge menacing furry black stamens, Viola had no doubt guessed in a trice that they were home grown, thereby cleverly endearing herself to two of her hosts with a single throw. Indeed, it turned out that Kitty was an expert gardener, though not, naturally, the kind who grubbed about on her knees, but very knowledgeable on Latin names, soil content and suchlike esoteric matters, and she offered to take Viola and myself on a brief, pre-lunch tour of the rose garden, among other highlights. Douglas was all for leaping on to his crutches and accompanying us, but she instructed him in sharp, peremptory tones to remain where he was and obey doctor's orders.

It struck me as I stared moodily at a *Vampirea dolorosa*, or some such plant which, we were informed, had been on the point of dying only a few weeks ago, but had miraculously, if misguidedly come to life again, that Viola might even have contrived to bestow still another favour by setting up this boring expedition. It had not sounded to me as though Kitty's refusal to allow her husband to take part in it had stemmed from a deep concern for his injured ankle. Her automatic and shrewish response had suggested that she was accustomed to prising him away from presentable females in whom he was showing an interest. Viola had certainly proved herself to be a valuable ally in round one, but, since we had at least another two hours to get through at Dene Cottage and Douglas was probably not the kind to be intimidated by wifely dis- approval, I could see storm clouds ahead unless I too could disarm her before we rejoined the party. So I began by saying what a shame it was that Toby was not here to enjoy all these wonders, even though they would have made him so envious. It was not a fortunate gambit, how- ever, because I could see from her blank look that she had not the faintest idea who I was referring to.

'Oh yes, of course,' she said, pulling herself together. 'Your husband! Yes, what a pity! But never mind, perhaps you'll be able to bring him another time.'

Her tone was so patronising that I longed to tell her that I would not inflict such an ordeal on my worst enemy, but most of my resentment was reserved for Viola. How tiresome of her, I told myself, not to have warned me that

Toby's invitation had been pure fiction, invented by herself in one of her frenzies of tact, in the full knowledge that she had little to fear, since he was almost bound to refuse. Kind and considerate she might be, but she was so intent on smoothing her own path through life that she did not care how many rocks and boulders she strewed over other people's. At that moment I almost believed her capable of murdering Melanie and leaving her to rot under a pile of chalk, simply to restore peace and harmony to the Rotunda.

However, when we had completed this tedious tour and Kitty had gone ahead of us into the house, on the pretext of rounding up what she called the people in the kitchen, Viola took my arm and told me how stylish I was looking and how grateful she was to me for tagging along, instead of leaving her stuck with that odious woman. So I cast my unworthy thoughts aside and made up my silent quarrel with her on the spot.

When we returned to the drawing room Charlie had vanished and the rest of the party was split into two pairs Jamie and Len were in earnest conversation by the window and Marcia was seated on the floor beside Douglas's footstool, her knees drawn up to her chin and yearning up at him with her round, inviting eyes. She more or less ignored the reappearance of Viola and myself, but got up, not too hurriedly, when Kitty came to summon us to the dining room, pulling her T-shirt down over the gap of bare flesh which separated it from her jeans. Kitty cast a sweeping glance of dislike in her direction and then moved on to break up the dialogue of the couple by the window.

Lunch was notable more for its trimmings and garnishes than its actual content. The table napkins had been tortured into damask water lilies and there were rose leaves in the finger bowls, but rather more rice than chicken in the main dish and only one of the three glasses at each place setting was in fact needed.

Douglas, inevitably, was given Viola on his right and me on his left; she had Charlie on her other side, while I got Marcia. Kitty, making a great song and dance about eight being such an awkward number, divided herself between Jamie and Len. Douglas received Viola's effusive praise of his house and grounds with becoming modesty and then resumed his flirtation with me, as though there had been no interruption.

'Shocking tales I've been hearing about you, Tessa!'

'Oh, no! So soon?'

'Crowther tells me your husband is a policeman.'

'Oh, I see! Well, that's no dark secret.'

'Is he really?' Marcia asked, joining in with a loud squawk of amusement. 'How frightfully funny! Does he stand in the middle of the road, waving his arms about?'

'Sometimes,' I admitted. 'When he needs a taxi.'

'And you'd better mind your manners, Marcia,' Douglas told her. 'I hear he's something very special and high up in the C.I.D. Is that right, Tessa?'

'Not very high yet. About half way up, I should say.'

'And was he with you when you discovered that poor girl my cousin had befriended?'

'Oh, Jamie told you about that too, did he? Well, no that was someone else, as it happens,' I replied, sparing Viola's feelings.

'Must have been a most unpleasant experience?'

'Yes, it was, but I didn't hang around, you know. Just one look and off.'

Viola had been keeping an anxious eye on me during this exchange and I felt sure that, like me, she had been wondering whether the subject of Melanie's murder would crop up. As I met her look, she gave me a barely per-

ceptible shake of the head and once again I found myself
becoming irritated by her pussyfooting tactics. In any
case, I could hardly pretend not to have heard when
Douglas said:

'Did you ever meet the girl?'

'Once. How about you?'

'Not even once. I kept well out of it. Padmore was
always on at me to warn Elfrieda, but I couldn't see what
right I had to interfere. He was worried stiff about it,
poor old fellow. All most unsuitable and bound to lead to
trouble, he said, and how right he was!'

'I think that's a bit sweeping,' I said, earning myself a
flash of disapproval from Viola. 'If all the delinquents and
undesirables had to pay for their misdemeanours with
their lives, the population of these islands would be pretty
thin on the ground.'

'Good thing too, if you ask me,' Marcia said. 'As you'd
agree if you'd ever taken a look at all those plebs swarm-
ing over the beach every summer weekend.'

On hearing this remark, Len put his spoon down with
a clatter, turning scarlet in the face, as though apoplexy
were about to set in, and Charlie drawled:

'Poor lookout for me, though. I'd be an orphan in no
time, what with Dad sailing so near the wind in his business deals and Mum buying sweet peas from the local
florist and passing them off as all her own work at the
flower show.'

It must have been the last straw for Viola that Kitty
now joined in the fray. In a voice of suppressed fury, she
said:

'How dare you say such a thing? That was most un-
called for, Charlie!'

'Sorry, Mum. Just my little joke, you know.'

'Then it was extremely poor taste and you ought to be
ashamed of yourself. In my opinion, you owe both me

and your father an apology; and our guests too. Do you hear me?'

Personally, I considered her foolish to keep banging away at it like this, because anyone could see that Charlie was already slightly ashamed of himself and she was only adding to the general embarrassment by making such a big production of it.

'Very well,' he said, striving to sound light-hearted. 'Here we go, then! Mother and Father, ladies and gentlemen, I apologise. I promise not to make a joke ever again; and while I'm about it, I'll apologise to Marcia, for casting these aspersions on her future parents-in-law. How's that?'

The brief silence which followed was broken by a screech of laughter on my left and then Viola, ever ready with her little carafe of oil for the turbulent waters, nipped in with some questions to her host concerning the presence or otherwise of fish in the stream which ran through his property.

'Plenty,' he replied, apparently quite unmoved by the recent fracas. 'We keep it stocked and we've even put up a little hut in the wood down there, so that our ladies could join us for picnics. Never gets used, though. I don't seem to find much time for fishing, even when both legs are functioning, and it bores Charlie to death, doesn't it, Marcia?'

'Yes, thank God,' she replied, with another trumpeting laugh, which trailed off into a giggle when Charlie, after flinging his napkin down on the table, got up and walked out of the room.

'Plenty of undercurrents swimming around in that little corner of rural England,' I remarked to Jamie on the drive back to Dearehaven. 'I hope your professional eyes and ears were on the alert?'

'Oh no, all far too commonplace and predictable,' he

97

replied in his most superior tone. 'There are thousands of families like that and they've been done to death. Self-made man; vulgar, climbing wife; weakling of a son, we've had it all before. What one looks for is some unexpected twist to shake the whole thing up and turn the situation on its head.'

Leaving aside the fact that whoever had made Douglas, it was certainly not himself, I personally considered that Jamie had overlooked something this time and that, despite his contemptuous dismissal of the Henshaws as theatrical fodder, the very element he mentioned had actually been present.

I did not point this out, however, lest I be overheard by Viola, who was in front with Len, and who had probably suffered enough unpleasantness for one day.

THIRTEEN

By the following morning Toby was still rattling around in the Royal Metropolitan, having been called on by Inspector Watson, when on the brink of departure, and served with a subpoena for Melanie's inquest at the Town Hall on Tuesday morning.

'Don't they want me as well?' I asked him.

'Funnily enough, no. I explained that you were far better at that sort of thing than I am, but he was not interested. So here I am, getting terribly behind with my work and now this horror hanging over me.'

'Oh well, only a couple more days,' I reminded him, 'and it will be a pure formality, you know. Just a couple of questions, then the medical evidence and they'll probably wind up with an adjournment.'

'And adjourned is where it is likely to remain, I imagine.'

'Shouldn't wonder. Did the Inspector give you any hints about what headway they were making?'

'Certainly not. Why should he take me into his confidence?'

'Not deliberately,' I explained. 'Inadvertently is the word I had in mind.'

'Well, it wasn't in my mind, I assure you. I don't possess your gift for drawing the inadvertent out of people, specially policemen. However, it would be logical to assume that they are concentrating their efforts on the young man she was seen on the cliff with, and the still, small voice of reason tells me that they have a fat chance of catching up with him.'

'I agree. The trouble is that, so far as I know, the only one who did see him was Jamie and the best description he could give was that he had fair hair and was wearing jeans. That's a big help, isn't it? He could be absolutely anywhere by now, wearing dark hair and a pink suit, for all we know. And he may not have been a local boy either; more likely someone she'd picked up with on an earlier adventure and kept in touch with. She'd been on the move quite a bit during her short lifetime, so there's no telling when and where they might have met.'

'Which makes me feel even more inflamed at being kept here forcibly for such a pointless exercise. In fact, I wonder they bother to have an inquest at all.'

'Don't be so pessimistic. Something interesting may emerge. In fact, I don't see how it can fail to and it's the medical evidence which I'm depending on you to listen to most carefully.'

'How ghoulish of you!'

'Not the gory details, I'm not concerned with them, but I would very much like to know whether she died before Elfrieda or after.'

'Yes, I can see that, but isn't it a foregone conclusion? If this young man was the one who did it, there must have been a gap of nearly twenty-four hours between the two, with Melanie first past the post.'

'But the fact that no one appears to have seen her after Jamie got that glimpse on the cliff path doesn't necessarily mean she was killed the same evening. The carrier bag, for instance, indicates that they were planning to spend at least some time on the beach and if one or both of them had wanted to go into hiding they could have spent the night, even two nights, in one of the caves. The chances of anyone seeing and recognising her in Rocky Cove were pretty remote.'

'So, in a mix-up of this kind, with ten thousand pounds at stake and assuming they can't establish the exact time, who would legally be assumed to have died first?'

'I don't know, Toby, and it's one of the fascinating aspects.'

'I don't know why. If the young man did kill her, it can hardly have been for the money.'

'If he did, and if the girl Jamie saw really was Melanie, not just someone who resembled her from a distance, and several other "ifs", along with those; so do please keep your ears pinned back and drink up every word.'

'You do think of some charming pastimes to while away my summer hols,' he commented gloomily.

Nevertheless, he did not fail me and by Wednesday evening the plot, so far as I was concerned, had thickened to a stew.

Melanie had not been sexually assaulted, but this was about the only obscenity which had not been inflicted on her. Her neck, along with numerous other bones, had been broken, these injuries being commensurate with falling from a great height, but they had not caused her death. This had been due to a blow on the back of the skull, which had been sustained before she went over the cliff.

The medical evidence also produced a couple more surprises. One was that immediately before her death she had consumed a massive amount of alcohol, the equivalent, when translated into layman's terms for the benefit of the jury, of four double whiskies. The other was that, by the Saturday morning when she was found, she had been dead for not less than five days, not longer than a week. In other words, she had been alive and well and probably living in Dearehaven for not less than four days after Elfrieda died.

'So what becomes of all the money she had inherited?' I asked, when the three of us gathered on Viola's terrace that evening. The question was addressed to Jamie, who had just returned from an emergency meeting at the Rotunda, with Roger Padmore once again in the chair, and was therefore well primed on recent developments.

'Since it is safe to assume that she died intestate,' he replied, 'I understand that the greater part of it will clatter into the coffers of the national exchequer.'

'And the smaller part?' Viola asked. 'Who gets that?'

'No idea, but at least she'll have the privilege of paying for her own funeral and legal expenses, poor girl. I daresay there'll be a thousand or two going begging when it's all wound up, and then they'll have to advertise for any relatives who may care to step along and hear something to their advantage. I gather that in a case of that sort countless people feel the urge to step along, but since most, if not all, will be charlatans, they will be wasting their shoe leather.'

'How about the Orphanage, though?' I suggested. 'Can't they dig up someone?'

'Not a vestige. She was that classic case of the almost new born baby dumped outside a police station in the dead of night. Not so much as a label pinned to her shawl, and they never found out where she came from. She was called Melanie Jones after the heroine of a novel the Matron of the Home happened to be hooked on at the time.'

'All the same,' I said, 'it's possible that she formed some kind of relationship of her own after she got away from there. She could even have made a will, for all we know.

102

There's a cheap kind of printed form which one can buy at a stationer's and it's perfectly legal.'

'Most unlikely,' Viola said. 'Even if she had known she was an heiress, and I agree that she probably did, disposing of her money when she was dead would have been the last thing to enter that young person's head. She'd have been putting her mind to spending it while she was alive. In any case, people of that age never believe they're going to die.'

'But supposing she'd got married, Viola? In that case, it wouldn't have been necessary to think about death, or make a will either. The money would pass automatically to her husband, wouldn't it?'

Jamie had evidently come to a tricky bit of shading in his tapestry, for he was holding it up to the light, tilting it this way and that and prodding it with his needle:

'Who said she was married?' he asked in an abstracted voice.

'No one, dear,' Viola assured him soothingly, 'Just another of Tessa's little flights of fancy. Take no notice.'

'I don't see why you should call it that,' I protested. 'People are doing it all the time and she was over the age of consent.'

'Well, it certainly introduees a new element,' Jamie said, 'which is something to be grateful for, perhaps. If I were you, Tessa, I'd pass that one on to the Inspector. He could easily turn up the records and find out if there was a marriage and then, as far as I can see, it would simply be a matter of finding the young man and arresting him for the murder of his bride. If he first married Melanie and then killed her to get his hands on her money, he won't get very far by concealing himself. In fact, it sounds to me as though he had behaved rather rashly.'

'Not necessarily,' I said. 'If he sticks to it that he has never been in Dearehaven and that Melanie had gone back there on her own to collect her belongings, then, so long as no witness could be found to prove otherwise, there'd be nothing much they could do about it. A motive of that kind would certainly be seized on by the prosecution, but I doubt if it would be enough. They'd need circumstantial evidence as well and, if he's a bright lad, he'll doubtless have fixed himself up with an alibi. Since the timing of her death gives a margin of forty-eight hours, that shouldn't present much of a problem.'

'The thing is that we always forget how well versed Tessa is in the complexities of crime, don't we, Viola? Was it Robin who suggested that Melanie might have a husband?'

'No, as a matter of fact, it was you.'

'Me? My darling girl, I promise you, such an idea never entered my head.'

'It was the way you described them, walking along the cliff. You said they were swinging along hand in hand. Somehow that didn't sound like a casual pick-up. More like two people who'd known each other for some time and liked what they knew.'

'It is possible to achieve that without wedding bells.'

'Yes, I know, but there was something else. You . . .' I began, but Viola was growing impatient.

'Why waste time arguing about it? As Jamie rightly says, if she had acquired a husband at some point in her varied career, there will be records to show who he was, but personally I can't see that it affects us, one way or another.'

'Although the verdict was wilful murder,' I pointed out, 'and if the young man Jamie saw her with didn't kill her, then someone else did, and I should have thought that mattered quite a lot.'

'In what way?'

'Well, listen, Viola, this is murder, as I say, and it won't just be wiped off the slate because the victim happened to be a rather troublesome nonentity. There'll be a full investigation and it could go on for months.'

'Let it. I don't care.'

'Nonsense, Viola, of course you care,' Jamie said, wagging his needle at her. 'I can see quite well what Tessa is getting at.'

'Then kindly explain.'

'What I'm getting at,' I told her, not over-keen to have my punch line snatched away, 'is simply this: since Melanie hadn't been raped or disfigured, it's probable that this wasn't the act of some drunken thug. More likely deliberate, committed for a purpose, and for that you need more than just a passing acquaintance with your victim. So just ask yourself who in Dearehaven, apart from Elfrieda, knew Melanie well enough to have such an urgent need to remove her?'

'Oh,' she muttered, looking perfectly appalled. 'Yes, I must admit that hadn't occurred to me . . . but it's utterly ridiculous.'

'Of course it is, but it remains a fact, nonetheless, and one which I promise you will not be overlooked. That painstaking investigation I referred to is going to be centred on the Rotunda and all the people who work there, so you'd better start getting used to the idea.'

FOURTEEN

The warning evidently had its effect, for it was not hard to recognise Viola's hand in the decision to send a wreath to Melanie's funeral, complete with a card bearing the inscription: 'With love and sympathy from all at the Rotunda Theatre'. Perhaps she was counting on its being seen by Inspector Watson, who would instantly realise that we had all been devoted to the deceased and that it would therefore be unnecessary to pester us with tiresome questions about whether we had any reason to wish her dead.

The cremation was to take place on Friday afternoon at three o'clock, a time which made it quite easy for all her loving and sympathetic friends to find adequate excuses not to attend. Unfortunately, though, this idea of the wreath had been arrived at rather late in the day and, in accepting the order, the florists declared themselves unable to complete and deliver it on time. The most they could promise was to have it ready for us to collect at one o'clock, when they closed for lunch. So someone had to take it from there to the crematorium and, after some further discussion, this task was allotted to me.

Although expressing herself somewhat hesitantly, Viola appeared to feel that, being a comparative newcomer and one who had scarcely known Melanie personally, I should not suffer the same emotional strain as would afflict the rest of them in performing this ceremony.

'I am perfectly willing to sacrifice my lunch hour to oblige you,' I told her, 'but don't go too far, please! I'm not such a dotty comparative newcomer as to be unaware that every single one of you hated her like poison. It's a bit thick to pretend that the sight of her last resting place would have you all in tears.'

'Well yes, exactly! That's more or less what I mean,' she explained uncomfortably. 'You can afford to be detached about it, naturally, but there would be something so bizarre about any of us turning up there with a wreath. One would feel such a ghastly hypocrite, if you see what I mean?'

I told her I did and she thanked me again and handed over the money that had been raised by the whip round. I reckoned that it might just about cover the cost of the wreath, or the taxi to the crematorium, which according to Len was discreetly located eight miles from the town centre, but certainly not both. However, luckily for me, Kyril's sentiments were not quite so delicate and he offered to drive me there in his car.

'Not wishing to sound ungrateful,' I told him, 'but if you're prepared to do that much, why not just deliver the damn thing yourself?'

'Oh no, that would be so odious and boring,' he replied in his lazy fashion. 'Besides, it would be impossible to get to the shop in time. I have someone coming to see me at noon and he is so often quite late. If you bring your bouquet to my flat, I shall give you something to fortify you and then I will take you there and wait for you in the car.'

'Okay, it's a deal, so long as you promise to get me back within the hour. Otherwise, I'll be in trouble with Len, which is the last thing I need. He's been in a frightful fluster these last few days. I suppose it dates from that dreadful shock of finding Elfrieda dead in her wheel-chair.'

Kyril responded to this with one of his pensive, melancholy looks, his eyes clouding over, as they invariably did when he appeared to be concentrating:

'Yes,' he agreed with a deep sigh, 'I had noticed it.'

It was a modern, vaguely ecclesiastical looking building, like so many of its kind, but departed from the norm by being set in a huge, meticulously tended garden, laid out with dozens of flower beds in every variety of size and shape. The macabre feature was that every single one was planted with roses, all now blooming in such magnificent profusion that they looked quite artificial. Not only macabre either, but somehow typical of Dearehaven and it was impossible not to wonder which of these gorgeous bushes was about to receive another shot in the arm, in the form of some more human ashes.

All was silent and deserted, not even a gardener or attendant in slight, indicating that the lunch hour was as strictly observed here as in the world of the living. I wished I had taken this contingency into account, for I was now in some dilemma as to how to dispose of my wreath. Looking about me, I saw an arrow pointing to the car park, evidently at the back of the building, so set off in that direction, in the hope of finding someone to guide me.

It contained only one car, which at the very moment of my rounding the corner began to move towards the exit. I flung up my free arm in an attempt to catch the driver's attention, but he either didn't notice or didn't want to know, for gathering speed all the time, he turned into the short, rose bordered drive down to the road and disappeared from sight.

However, by this time my eye had been caught by something else of much more practical value. Stacked against the chapel wall and quite close to where I was standing was a large pile of wreaths and cellophane wrapped flowers. I read the card on one of them and learnt that it had come, with deepest sympathy, from Cis and Norman. Resisting the temptation to toss my own tribute on to this collection, I walked on a little further and was rewarded by the sight of what could only be its proper destination.

This second pile was much smaller and contained only three offerings, but one of them provided all the clue I needed, since it was a bunch of singularly repellent looking mauve tulips. Although there was no card attached and it was surprising to find them there at all, there could be no doubt of their having been sent by the Henshaw family.

Next to this was a cross shaped wreath, mainly composed of laurel leaves, the gift of the Matron and Staff of the Brackley Place Children's Home, but the third offering was in complete contrast to its shabby companions. It was a small, white, basket shaped vase, filled with miniature pink roses. There was something a little sad and touching about it. Mysterious too, for it also bore no card.

Kyril was slumped in his seat with his chin on his chest when I returned to the car, and gave the impression of being in a deep slumber. This was a setback, because I had intended to put him through an observation test, although I should have remembered how short sighted he was, or pretended to be, and how unlikely, asleep or awake, to be of much use.

'Tell me something,' I said climbing in beside him, 'did you see a car come out of here a few minutes ago?'

He was fiddling with a bunch of about twenty keys,

searching for the one for the ignition, and took his time:

'Yes, now you mention it, I believe there was one.'

'Did you recognise it?'

'No. Why? Should I have?'

'I'm not sure. I only saw it from a distance, but it looked familiar to me.'

'So? Whose do you think it was?'

'Len's.'

'Really? And was Len driving it?'

'Presumably, although I was too far off to see. What do you suppose he could have been doing there?'

'Nothing, my dear. I don't believe for a moment that he was there. You were mistaken, that's all; but if it bothers you so much, why not ask him?'

'Because, whether it were true or not, he would deny it. I was hoping you'd be my witness.'

'And I must regretfully disappoint you. All cars look alike to me. And why should he deny it? He may go where he chooses, I suppose?'

'Yes, but he obviously wouldn't want anyone to know about this. Otherwise, why didn't he offer to take the blasted wreath himself, instead of thrusting it on to me?'

'Why, indeed? Which, for me, is enough proof that you were mistaken. You do not make sense, you see, *ma chère* Tessa. How could he have gone there, hoping to keep it a secret, when he knew that you would also be coming and would be bound to see him?'

'It's a question of timing, Kyril. You see, Len knew that I'd ordered a taxi at ten minutes to one, to take me to the florists and then on, but that's all he knew. Naturally, he would assume that I'd collect the flowers, go to the crematorium and straight back into town again, stopping for only two minutes to shed my load. The whole operation wouldn't have taken more than forty minutes at the outside, so by setting out himself at one-thirty he'd have felt quite safe.'

'Oh well, yes, that is true, I suppose.'

'If it was he, I imagine he must have been a bit put out to find no wreath from the Rotunda, but maybe he concluded that I'd handed it over to someone in charge. Perhaps he was only pretending not to see me waving like a lunatic? Perhaps he knew quite well who I was, realised the timetable had gone wrong and shot off in panic? The more I think of it, the more certain I become that it was his car.'

'Never mind! Why worry about it? He was not committing any crime.'

'But don't you find it curious, Kyril?'

'Not so much as you.'

'Why not?'

He became silent for a minute or two, as though debating with himself, and finally he said:

'If I tell you what I believe is the explanation, you must promise not to say a word to Lennie, or anyone at all. It is all over now, all in the past.'

While privately regarding this statement as somewhat optimistic, I did not interrupt and he went on:

'You must have noticed by now that Len is very demented about his work. It is the great love of his life and I would even say that it means more to him than any human being, man or woman.'

'You could well be right, but what's that got to do with it?'

'Silence, please, and let me finish! He is also, as so often in affairs of the heart, very jealous and insecure, always terrified that someone is going to spring out and snatch his beloved away from him. As you will also have noticed, he is inclined to be over-emotional and impulsive and this

111

sometimes gets him into trouble and creates misunderstandings.'

'Which is more or less what you are creating now, but go on!'

'Well, this is what happened with Melanie. When she first came along some of us were quite amused and we did our best to like her and teach her some good manners and so on; also something about the theatre, which she pretended to be so crazy about, but no one tried harder in this way than Len. You understand?'

'Beginning to.'

'Well, of course after some while most of us gave up. One saw through her and ceased to be amused. Also she did not need us. She may have had these dreams of becoming the big star, but she did not intend to achieve it by hard work. Influence would do more for her, she thought, but of course Elfrieda was completely taken in. She never knew the score and neither, in a sense, did Len.'

'You imply that he went on helping her in order to do himself a bit of good with Elfrieda?'

'Oh, that is too blunt! Perhaps we should say that he found it easier to like her because this would please Elfrieda. He worked hard at it, too, poor boy. Took her to these film society shows and made her learn bits of Shakespeare and walk up and down with a pile of books on her head. You know?'

'So well.'

'And yet, although it began in that way, I feel there was some affection as well. She did not lack a certain charm, you know, and she had vitality and high spirits. Len is the withdrawn, moody kind, so maybe it was an attraction of opposites.'

'And you think that could have induced him to go there this morning? To say goodbye, as it were?'

'I do think it's possible, if he had become a little bit

112

attached to her, and also perhaps because of some feelings of remorse that he had not tried harder, now that she had died in this horrible way. Being so introspective, he might now feel that he had used her in just the same way as she had used Elfrieda. So now you understand, Tessa, why this is such a sensitive subject, and why you should keep perfectly quiet about what you saw?'

I agreed to this, although making private reservations in the case of Robin and Toby, and in a somewhat distrait fashion, for I had much on my mind.

Quite apart from the revelations about Melanie, which were beginning to crop up on all sides, it had not escaped me that, having started by scorning my suggestion that Len had been at the crematorium, Kyril had then turned right round and produced a complete set of credible reasons to show that I had been right. Credible, that is, but not wholly convincing, for it had also occurred to me that it would have needed a very severe attack of remorse to have prompted Len to make this secret, solitary pilgrimage to a place which must have filled him with loathing and horror. Moreover, remorse was not an emotion which one readily associated with that charmingly sentimental little vase of pink roses.

FIFTEEN

Nothing occurred during the afternoon rehearsal session either to disprove or confirm Kyril's allegations. It was true that Jamie had chosen this occasion to be present, but, although unusual, this was not unique and it could have been sheer imagination on my part that there was something specially wary and watchful in his behaviour, such as one might expect from a dramatist whose fledgling director was going through an emotional crisis.

Unfortunately, as I knew from experience, his presence on its own, watchful or otherwise, was enough to precipitate an emotional crisis and the fact that Len continually lost his place in the script, changed his mind from one minute to the next, was querulous and facetious by turns and pulled his hair about until it looked like an old floor mop, did not necessarily indicate that part of his mind was on a funeral service, which was taking place only eight miles away.

So when this painful session had at last come to an end and Viola and I were on our way home, I decided to try her out on the subject and, with no beating about the bush, asked her whether there was any truth in the rumour that Len and Melanie had been more than just bad friends. It has to be acknowledged that this was in direct contravention to the undertaking I had given Kyril, but I thought very little of that. If what he had said was true, then he cannot have been the only one to have known about it and, although Viola may not have been the most observant woman to be encountered in a day's march, it was unlikely to come as red hot news to her.

However, I was prepared to protect Kyril up to a point and when she replied to my question with one of her own, to the effect that she would be interested to hear where I had picked up such an extraordinary notion, I said:

'Nowhere in particular. Something about the way he spoke of her the first time I met him gave me the idea that he might be slightly bitten. Was I wrong?'

It seemed to me that I was continually trying to get people to part with information while they were driving cars and that this gave them an unfair advantage. Evidently, they could not be expected to keep up a steady flow of conversation while also required to watch the traffic lights, change gear and wait to see whether that idiot in front was really going to turn right. I could almost hear the thoughts buzzing through Viola's head as she applied herself to these tasks, but unfortunately there was no way of telling whether her words, which ultimately took the form of yet another question, accurately reflected them.

'Hasn't it occurred to you, Tessa, that Len's tastes lie in a somewhat different direction?'

'I thought he was a bit indeterminate, if you really want to know.'

'In what way?'

'Well, you know, no hard and fast preferences, capable of falling in love with just about anyone, irrespective of age or sex. For instance, I realise he's got a slight crush on Jamie, but he was also undeniably potty about Elfrieda.'

115

'That's rather different, dear.'

'I know, I only meant that he's obviously got a great deal of love and affection to fling about, it's practically spilling over and that a little bit of it might have overflowed on to Melanie. However, you obviously don't agree?'

'Oh, I wouldn't go as far as that,' Viola answered, carefully negotiating the turn on to the cliff road. 'I hadn't thought of it in quite those terms before, but there could be something in it. I do know that he was giving her some coaching at one point. One more or less took it for granted that he was doing it on instructions from Elfrieda, but when you think of it, she would hardly have ordered him to do that. So maybe it was entirely his own idea and the desire to do himself a bit of good with Elfrieda was only incidental. Now, be an angel and open the garage door for me, will you?'

It struck me as I performed this angelic task that this was the second time in an afternoon that my suggestion of there being some special relationship between Len and Melanie had met first with a stern rebuttal and only minutes later with the admission that, perhaps after all, there could be some truth in it.

The trouble was that I could not be sure whether this was because I had been clever enough to wring these concessions from both Kyril and Viola, against their better judgement, or whether they had been clever enough to fob me off with a half truth, the better to conceal the whole one. So I decided to seek information elsewhere.

Enquiries in the town had elicited the news that the Brackley Place Children's Home had been founded, endowed and, in his lifetime, virtually governed by Elfrieda's great uncle, Joseph Henshaw. Although nowadays subject to all the rules and controls of the Welfare Department, it was still a registered charity, existing mainly on voluntary contributions.

In the early days its doors had been opened to sixty orphaned boys and girls, aged from infancy to fourteen years and, with that celebrated Victorian blend of high philanthropy and low cunning, Joseph had laid it down that, along with the three R's and a heavy dose of religious instruction, every inmate should be trained in domestic service.

In compliance with modern prejudice, this condition had now been dropped, but there was still a domestic science course open to those who wished to take it and Mrs Banks, of the Green Man, who was my principal informant in these matters, told me that it was probably an above average one. She and her husband had several times taken on apprentices and part time workers from the Home during the summer season and most of them had turned out well.

'You wouldn't happen to remember the Matron's name?' I asked her and, luckily, it was unusual enough for her to have no difficulty in recalling it. She was called Mrs Bracegirdle and I rang her up and made an appointment to call on her the following day, introducing myself, just in case she had seen my name in the advance publicity, as Mrs Robin Price.

Brackley Place, as I then discovered, was set slightly back from the Dearehaven–Dorchester road and, fortunately for me, was on a bus route. This also helped to explain how Melanie had been able to run away with such regularity.

From the outside it was unexpectedly attractive, consisting of one medium sized house and six or eight bungalows, each with its own garden, grouped around it and separated from each other by grass and trees.

It had not taken long to hit on what I regarded as an adequate pretext for this visit and I had explained on the telephone that I was engaged on the official biography of Elfrieda and was in search of material for it.

Evidently, it had not occurred to Mrs Bracegirdle, who was a stout, fair haired woman with brilliant false teeth, that whichever officials had appointed me had been remarkably quick off the mark and, better still, she showed no curiosity whatever about my previous work in this field. She was intensely proud of her establishment and her single concern was to leave me in no doubt about the non-institutional, free and easy and humanitarian fashion in which it was run, extolling the happy results which had been achieved during her administration by splitting the children into small groups, each supervised by its own house mother and so creating not just one, but half a dozen happy families. After a while one began to feel quite sorry for children who were brought up in ordinary homes by their own parents.

However, I also had my bus to think about, so I assured her that everything she had told me would be scrupulously reported in the book, but that I was also anxious to place it in relation to the late Elfrieda.

'I daresay you have quite a few personal memories?' I asked her. 'Did she often visit you?'

'Well no, not so much in my time. She suffered dreadfully from arthritis, as I expect you know, and I've only been here the eight years. Not wishing to boast, there've been a good many improvements since then, though I do say it.'

'Yes, I can tell, but Miss Henshaw still took an interest in the place, I gather?'

'Oh, she did indeed, she was a real friend to us. Always

118

giving charity performances at her theatre to raise money for something extra we needed and the children were given seats for the panto every Boxing Day matinée, without fail. She was a real old darling.'

'So you're going to miss her?'

'You can say that again! And not only for that sort of thing, either. She was a wonder at finding good foster parents. One or two of them have even come back for more.'

'And I understand she took one of them in herself?'

Mrs Bracegirdle looked puzzled: 'No, I can't call to mind her doing that. Not in my time, anyway.'

'I was thinking of that poor girl who was found murdered on the beach the other day. She was one of yours, wasn't she?'

'Oh, Melanie Jones! Yes, I see what you mean. Miss Henshaw did take her under her wing, that's true, and much thanks she got for it, by all accounts; but that was a bit different. It was years after Melanie left here.'

'But she was here in your day?'

'For a year or two. She must have been ten or eleven when I first came and, to tell you the truth, Mrs Price, I hate to say this about any kiddie, but I wasn't all that sorry to see the back of her.'

'So no foster parents there?'

She sighed: 'We did our best. She had her chance, same as the others. Two of them, in fact, but the hard truth is that Melanie was one of our few failures.'

'What happened?'

'She had a couple of trial periods. Some families prefer that, you know. They don't want what you might call permanencies, but they're willing to take a child for a few weeks and then, if it works out well, they make a regular thing of it. Not always a very satisfactory arrangement, to my mind; a bit unsettling, if you know what I mean, but in Melanie's case it did a lot more harm than good, on both sides.'

'Why was that?'

'Because she was Melanie, I suppose. Probably couldn't help herself, poor kid, but she had such grand ideas. Forever boasting and carrying on to the other children about how she came from a very aristocratic family, and I don't know what all. Anyway, we thought it might do her good to spread her wings a bit and a nice, middle-aged couple took her in one summer. They had a child of their own, but he was nearly old enough to go to college by then and they liked the idea of having somebody young about the place. Kind, decent people they were, and doing their best, but ordinary, if you take my meaning? He had a chemist's shop in the High Street. Did very well out of it, too, but that wasn't half grand enough to suit Miss Melanie Jones, oh dear me, no. You'd never believe how she behaved. Criticising their table manners, turning up her nose at their friends, a proper little monkey she was. I'm sorry to have to say such things, seeing what's happened to her, but there it is and, naturally enough, they weren't keen to repeat the experiment.'

'So where did she go the next time?'

'Well, that wasn't until a year or two later. It was all Miss Henshaw's doing and it'll give you an idea of the sort of person she was. "Very well", she says. "If the silly girl thinks she's so superior, let's give her a chance to put it to the test", and she actually got round some very rich people to take Melanie in one Easter time. Goodness knows how she managed it, because I'm sure they'd never have dreamt of such a thing, left to themselves, but there you are! That was Miss Henshaw all over. Once she'd set her mind on something she usually got her own way. I'm sure a lot of people will tell you that.'

'They already have. So she knew Melanie as long ago as that?'

'Oh well, only by her case history, so to speak. I doubt if there was anything personal in it. We never have less than forty children here and a good number of them are ships that pass in the night. It's unlikely she'd have been able to put a face to any one name.'

'And I gather this second visit was a flop too? What went wrong this time?'

'That was worse than ever, in a sense. At least, with the others she'd just been silly and showing off, but the second time it ended with her being packed off back here in disgrace.'

'Why? What had she done?'

'Stolen some money, if you please! The lady of the house caught her in the act. I must say that was a real blow. I suppose it was being surrounded by so much luxury which did it, but to be fair I'd never thought her capable of that sort of thing. Naughty and rebellious yes, but not dishonest. Anyway, that was the end of it and we didn't try again. In fact, it wasn't long afterwards that she first ran away and what a lot of trouble that led to! Of course she had her good points too, I don't deny it. She was full of bright ideas, some of them too bright by half, and she was crazy about play acting, always organising the others into getting up entertainments. Quite clever some of them were too, but she always had to be the one to shine and she wanted to keep all the best parts for herself. Proper little show off, as I say.'

I would have encouraged her to say more, but my bus was almost due and there was still one question to be asked:

'You've been so kind,' I began, 'and I'm wondering if I dare ask you to help me in just one more way?'

'I'll do my best, Mrs Price, so long as you promise to

give us a nice write-up in your book. What was it you wanted to know?'

'I was hoping you might be able to give me the address of those people, the chemist and his wife, who had Melanie to stay? You see, facts and dates and so on are relatively easy to come by, but what I'm digging for is anecdotes. It's fair to assume that Miss Henshaw interviewed this couple personally, at least once, before the visit was fixed up and it would be awfully useful to hear some of their memories of her.'

'Oh, there now, what a shame!' Mrs Bracegirdle said, sounding genuinely regretful. 'Sorry dear, I'm afraid you've stumped me this time. They moved away from here a year or two ago and that shop has been pulled down now. It's all these multiple stores. I suppose you could make some enquiries at the post office? There might be some record of a forwarding address?'

'Yes, thank you, I'll try that, and in the meantime . . .'

'Yes?'

'The other family you mentioned? Are they still around, by any chance?'

She hesitated, looking dubious for the first time, but then, apparently overcoming her scruples, she said:

'Well, I really can't see any reason for not telling you. They wouldn't mind now, after all these years, and you're bound to come across them, anyway.'

'Oh, am I? Why's that?'

'Because they're relations of Miss Henshaw, you see! Mr and Mrs Douglas. Sir Douglas, as he is now.'

SIXTEEN

'So that was the end of that jolly little masquerade,' Robin said, having arrived later that evening and heard my description of the visit to Brackley Place, during dinner at the Green Man.

'Looks like it,' I admitted. 'I can't very well go capering over to Dene Cottage and present myself as Mrs R. Price, who has been commissioned to write the official biography. But what do you make of it, Robin? When we had lunch there last Sunday and the subject of Melanie came up, Douglas flatly denied having met her.'

'Probably didn't make the connection. It was a long time ago, after all, and I daresay he'd hardly given her a thought since then.'

'Even so, I bet you it would have all come floating back when he read about the murder. Melanie Jones is not a name you hear every day of your life, is it? I think it's more likely that he knew exactly who she was and didn't want to admit it.'

'So now, I suppose, you are working on a lovely story of the ten-year-old Melanie mastering the combination of the Henshaw safe, clawing around with her baby fingers for bundles of cash and coming across some incriminating documents, which she has been using to blackmail Douglas ever since?'

'Quite right, Robin, that's exactly what I am doing.'

'Rather young for such sophisticated practices, wasn't she?'

'Well, it's only your idea that she was ten at the time. In fact, Mrs Bracegirdle told me that it was soon afterwards that she ran away, so she must have been at least thirteen by then and probably precocious with it.'

'All the same, you'd have a job to prove anything.'

'I'll keep at it.'

'Yes, I expect you will,' he sighed, 'but in the meantime there are more pressing matters requiring your attention. Have you been able to lay on some golf for me tomorrow morning?'

'Certainly, I have. It's all fixed up with Jamie. He'll take you there in person and introduce you.'

'Jamie's a member?'

'Not an active one. He joined it so as to be free to march about all over the course whenever he chooses. Also, from a professional standpoint, he likes to sit in the clubhouse and eavesdrop on the playing members' conversation. He says it can be very weird and fascinating.'

'I must see if I can't tune in myself,' Robin said, 'and bring some home for you.'

For a beginner he didn't do badly, but then it must be said that he had more than his share of beginner's luck.

In the first place, Jamie, who was famous enough for his company to be eagerly sought in the higher social echelons and knew everyone who was worth knowing, introduced him to Colonel Meyrick, the local Chief Constable, on the assumption that they would have much in common, besides a shared dedication to that footling game.

Knowing a little by now of Jamie and his methods, I could hazard the guess that he was grinding an axe of his own in bringing them together, but did not object to this, since he was also grinding mine in the process.

The truth was that, despite my solemn warning to Viola, we had been sadly neglected by the police in the matter of Melanie's murder. Apart from taking brief statements from everyone at the Rotunda, to establish when he or she had last seen her alive, they had left us severely alone and we were quite in the dark as to what, if any, line of investigation they were pursuing.

Viola, understandably, was inclined to be smug about this, taking it as clear proof that they had already admitted defeat and were content to drop the case into the file labelled 'Unsolved' and forget about it, but I guessed that Jamie did not believe this, any more than I did. His first question every evening when he arrived on the terrace was whether either of us had heard any news and now, no doubt bored and frustrated by our regular negative responses, had seized on Robin as the tool to prise some information from the most reliable horse of all, in the knowledge that Colonel Meyrick would open his mouth more freely to a fellow professional than to a member of the public, even one who was a national celebrity.

The assumption was correct, although the upshot rather on the negative side, which, paradoxically, accounted for Colonel Meyrick's readiness to disclose it. It had been in his mind for some while to ask for assistance from Scotland Yard and this friendly, unofficial session with one of its members was in the nature of a dry run, not committing him to a full scale performance. His indecision stemmed from the fact that what had begun by looking like a perfectly straightforward act of violence committed by a drunken hooligan and only unintentionally ending in homicide, was now turning out to be a good deal more complicated.

A major snag was that, although two people claimed to have seen Melanie in Dearehaven, on two separate occasions, about a week before her death, after a whole week of painstaking enquiry, the number still remained at two. Furthermore, equally painstaking enquiries in the local pubs and discos had not produced a single witness to testify having served or noticed a young couple of that description in a state of intoxication. Moreover, if the girl Jamie and I saw really had been Melanie, then she had apparently surfaced in the town for a brief period, left it and returned again approximately forty-eight hours later, since not a single trace of her had been found during the interval.

The alternative, which opened up some disturbing possibilities, was that she had been engaged in some unlawful activity, with an accomplice, who, having no criminal record, had been able to provide her with a hiding place where no one would ever dream of searching. In that case, the accomplice would have to be either someone quite unknown to the police or else someone nearer home who had been interrogated and had lied.

'So what are they doing about it?' I asked.

'Oh, plastering the local television news with photographs, requesting any viewer who saw this girl to step forward, that kind of routine stuff. There's not much else they can do. In fact, if you want my candid opinion, they've more or less reached a stalemate.'

'And if they do call in the Yard, perhaps you'll be put in charge of the case.'

'It's a bare possibility, I suppose. Since you didn't appear at the inquest and only met the girl once, in a crowd of other people, I daresay there'd be no ethical objection.'

'That'd be fun.'

126

'Think so? Not my idea of fun. There's nothing more depressing than taking on a case with the scent as cold as yesterday's mutton and no leads at all.'

'Oh well, with a little help from me, you know!'

'And how many leads have you got?'

'One or two. Enough, anyway, to convince me that they're right about her having an accomplice, although that isn't quite the word I'd have used. Protector would be more like it.'

'Guess or knowledge?'

'Deduction. She vanished into nowhere on two separate occasions and it wasn't as though she was a stranger in these parts. Scores of people round here must have known her by sight. I don't see how she could have managed it without assistance from someone.'

'None of which brings us any nearer to finding out who it was.'

I did not entirely agree with him there and, although refraining from saying so aloud, must have betrayed it in my expression, for he said:

'And just in case you're still clinging to that weird theory of Douglas Henshaw being the villain of the piece, I had better pass on another item I picked up this morning.'

'Concerning Douglas?'

'Yes, he really has been immobilised for these past few weeks. The broken ankle is perfectly genuine. It happened right there on the golf course, when his ball went into the rough. It was while hunting around for it that he caught his foot in a rabbit hole and went crashing down, in full view of three other members. He was in such a bad way that one of them drove him straight to his doctor.'

'Who said: "Yes, bad luck, old chap, a very nasty sprain! I'll just put this bandage on and you'd better try and rest it as much as you can for the next day or two."

I don't find the rabbit hole story at all convincing. In fact, it was the improbability of that broken ankle which gave me the idea in the first place that Douglas was somehow involved, even before I learnt that he was lying when he said he had never met Melanie. I simply don't believe that doctors allow their patients to dictate to them about whether their broken bones should go into plaster or not. I think they have ways of making them do what's good for them.'

'All the same, you can't seriously believe that Melanie was blackmailing him and what other conceivable motive could he have had for pushing her over a cliff?'

'Well, at the risk of being a bore, it all hinges on the original premise, which you and Toby found so hilarious, that Elfrieda's death was not quite so natural as it might have been.'

'You imply that Douglas gave her a push?'

'In a word, yes.'

'Why?'

'For the most commonplace of all reasons.'

'Oh, surely that's unlikely, Tessa? I agree he probably knew he was her principal heir, and it's also on the cards that he expected to inherit a much more sizeable chunk than he actually got, but from the way you described the style they live in, he's not exactly hard up, even without Elfrieda's money. Why suddenly become in such a desperate hurry to get his hands on it? If things had taken their natural course, he probably wouldn't have had to wait more than a year or two, in any case.'

'Perhaps he was scared she would change her will in favour of Melanie; or perhaps word had reached him that she was eating into her capital to prop up the Rotunda? In a year or two there might have been nothing left except a heavily mortgaged theatre. And I don't see that their putting on such a show at Dene Cottage is anything to go by. In the sort of world where Douglas operates a front of that kind would be essential to the image. If he sold off some of the land or sacked a couple of gardeners the word would soon get around that he was on the topple, which would probably be disastrous.'

'Yes, there's a grain of truth in that, I daresay, but it doesn't prove he's on the financial rocks, any more than the frugal life is a guarantee of financial stability.'

'I realise that, but I caught a whiff of something dubious during that ghastly lunch. Charlie, the son, made a rather feeble, fairly spiteful joke about his parents. He accused his mother of cheating at the flower show and the phrase he used about his father was that he sailed near the wind in business deals. The funny thing is that I feel sure it really was meant as a joke, because he'd hardly have said such a thing in front of a bunch of strangers if he believed it to be true, but it was Kitty who gave the game away. She completely lost her temper and wouldn't let it rest until he'd apologised.'

'And what was Douglas's reaction?'

'I can't tell you, I was watching Kitty. We were all mesmerised by her performance. But I doubt if it would have made much difference. Douglas is too cool a customer to betray himself by so much as a flicker.'

'So now we have a new variation on the same theme? Melanie was not blackmailing him for something she'd found out all those years ago, but because she saw him give Elfrieda the fatal shove?'

'Well, why not? And it needn't have been for money, either. That was a risk she didn't have to take, since she knew she had plenty coming her way. It might just have been revenge. Holding the threat of exposure over him to get her own back for the humiliation he'd caused her as a child. And a pretty nice revenge it would have been. Douglas could never have come out of a scandal of that kind unscathed. He'd have done anything to shut her up. Unfortunately for her, she didn't realise just how far he would go.'

Robin was silent for a moment or two and then came up with the one question which told me that he had begun to take the argument seriously:

'Just suppose there was something in this,' he asked, 'would it have been possible for Douglas to have got into the theatre and up to Elfrieda's office, without being seen, recognised and remembered?'

'Oh, any amount of ways,' I replied without hesitation, without, in fact, having given a thought to what they might have been.

'Such as?'

'Well, let's see now! Assuming he'd gone in through the front of the house, he could probably have just walked through to the ramp with no questions asked, so long as he did it in a confident, debonair sort of way. She had business appointments with all sorts of people every day and there would have been no reason to suppose that one of them had called for the express purpose of murdering her. What you have to remember is that there has never been a breath of suspicion surrounding Elfrieda's death, and so no one has ever been questioned about who they saw or what they were doing during the crucial period. When they do call in Scotland Yard and you take over the case, here's my advice: drop the Melanie end of it, for the time being, and concentrate on what they were all doing when Elfrieda took that tumble.'

SEVENTEEN

I was never to know whether he would have followed this advice or not because, alas for my high hopes, within twenty-four hours of this conversation, the proposed appeal for help from Scotland Yard went into abeyance once more, the local C.I.D. having got their first sight of a break-through, which led them straight to, of all people, Jill Sandford, our stage manager.

It came about from the fact that a certain Mr Paul Hockling had left for a holiday in Majorca on the very day that Melanie was found on the beach, not returning until two weeks later, and no computer had been able to supply the information which he alone possessed.

He had not seen any English newspapers while abroad, but it is unlikely that it would have made any difference if he had, for the girl whose face appeared on the screen of his television set on the day after his return home had been known to him as Jill Sandford.

Paul Hockling was manager and sole cashier of a tiny branch of one of the big banks, or rather of two such, and they were seven miles apart. The one at Brackley was open for business on Mondays, Wednesdays and Fridays and its humbler counterpart at Hawkham on Tuesdays and Thursdays. It was at the latter, a month or two before her death, that he had first encountered Melanie Jones, alias Jill Sandford, when she had applied to him to open a deposit account.

She had brought a driving licence for purposes of identification and, by way of reference, a letter on Rotunda writing paper, stating that she was employed there as stage manager and signed by the secretary to the General Administrator. She also paid in an initial deposit of one hundred pounds in cash, so was welcomed with fairly open arms, although Mr Hockling did express some curiosity as to her choosing such an out of the way spot to keep it in. Her reply to this was that she was staying in the neighbourhood, so Hawkham was just as convenient for her as Dearehaven.

During the ensuing weeks she had paid in regular sums of between twenty and a hundred pounds, explaining that these were the unspent balance from her salary and that she was saving up to get married. The amounts had, without exception, been paid in over the counter in cash, which had also aroused faint misgivings in the Hockling mind. He had pointed out that the usual procedure was to deposit the salary cheque and draw out such cash as was needed. She had countered this by saying that, although a perfect fool about money herself, someone who understood these things had told her that if she did as Mr Hockling suggested, hers would be in what they called a current account and would not be earning interest. In fact, there had been no withdrawals and at the time of her death she had a credit of over a thousand pounds.

Not surprisingly, when the real Jill Sandford stood up, Mr Hockling firmly denied ever having set eyes on her and, on unearthing the reference letter from the Rotunda, the signature was found to be that of M. Jones.

'Rather daring and clever,' I told Robin, when we had finished weaving together our separate strands of information during the evening telephone call. 'If the manager had decided to check it, the chances are that he would have rung up and asked to speak to Miss Jones, who would have been happy to assure him that all was in order and above board. Everything one learns about Melanie makes it increasingly clear that there was a lot more to her than met the eye. First we hear that Len had fallen under her spell and now this!'

'Didn't do her much good, poor girl! But I suppose you now feel vindicated in your blackmail theory?'

'How else could she have got her hands on all that money? She wasn't paid a salary, in cash or otherwise. All she had was pocket money doled out by Elfrieda. And we're getting warmer, you notice, Robin?'

'Warmer?'

'Hawkham, where she banked it, is only a mile or two from that stately Cottage of Dene.'

'In that case, I don't agree that it strengthens your case against Douglas, quite the reverse, in fact. If he'd been paying her hush money, that would have been the last place she'd have chosen.'

'I suppose you're right,' I admitted, 'and it may be just coincidence, because it's also very near the Home where she was brought up. Did your Chief Constable tell you whether the police have formed any theory of their own about where the money came from?'

'No, but the chances must be that it was from a local source. Wads of cash like that could hardly have been sent through the post. That's one up to you, I admit, but, all the same, if Douglas were involved in any way, it couldn't be on account of Elfrieda's death. The payments started long before that.'

'I still can't help believing that he comes into it somewhere. It's too much of a coincidence that he should have known her as a child . . .' I broke off here, adding in a brisk voice, 'Okay, then, I'll think it over and call you back,' trusting to luck that Robin would realise that, through the open doorway, I had just seen Jamie walk on to the terrace.

I had not been expecting him because it was now well past his usual calling time and he must have known that Viola would already have left for the theatre. I concluded that I had judged correctly in attributing him with an ulterior motive in bringing Robin and the Chief Constable together and had snatched this opportunity to come and get his reward in private. So I did the honours with the champagne and tapestry and waited to see how he would go about it.

He began by enthusing over the way my performance was working out and saying how absolutely right and marvellous I was going to be. However, this did not elevate me to the dizzy heights because it was exactly the line I would have taken if I had been hoping to extract some information out of someone who was not burning to part with it, and the next helping of flattery was fairly predictable too. Having asked me whether Robin would be able to get down for the first night, he re-threaded his needle, saying:

'What a dear fellow he is! And so attractive! You must be dotty about him.'

'Oh, I am.'

'And clever with it, so I hear.'

'Yes, I believe so.'

'Even my buffy old friend, Billy Meyrick, who is not given to superlatives, was wildly impressed. I gather they got on like a couple of bugs in the rug. Did Robin tell you?'

'Yes, he did, and also that it was very sweet and thoughtful of you to arrange it.'

I could not swear that those were Robin's exact words, but they were near enough for the purpose.

'Oh, nonsense! No trouble at all and I guessed they'd have a lot in common.'

'Yes, indeed, and apparently their handicaps are about the same too, which was very lucky. You've nearly finished that piece of work, haven't you? How many will that make altogether?'

'Four,' he replied, frowning at it and, considering that he had now been teased enough, I said:

'I gather Colonel Meyrick wasn't very forthcoming on the subject of Melanie, but that was because there wasn't much to come forth about.'

'Oh, really?' he replied, with a fine enough show of indifference to suggest that he might not have been such a bad actor as he had claimed.

'No, at that point they'd reached a dead end, if you'll forgive the pun?'

'Seeing as it's you; but why do you say "at that point"?'

'Simply because this business of the mysterious bank account has now jerked them into life again, even if it should turn out to be a short-lived one.'

Jamie laid down his work and gave me his undivided attention.

'What mysterious bank account?'

'You mean you haven't heard about poor old Jill being hauled off to the police station, to be identified by Mr Hockling?'

'Not a word. What had poor old Jill done?'

'Nothing. They turned her loose in five minutes, but you can imagine the stark terror. I'm surprised you hadn't heard.'

'No reason to be. I haven't been near the theatre today

135

and I haven't been at home much either. So let me put it another way; what was poor old Jill mistakenly thought to have done?'

'She was a mere pawn in someone else's game,' I explained and then proceeded to give him the full story, not forgetting to acknowledge that most of the inside information had come, via Robin, from the Chief Constable.

However, this did not have so gratifying an effect as I had hoped and as I went along I was saddened to notice that his expression changed from mild astonishment, through incredulity to fear and anger. I had never before seen him at a loss for words, but when I reached the climax, which was Melanie's secret hoard having passed the one thousand mark, his reaction reached such a pitch that I thought he would choke.

'Did you say a thousand, Tessa?' he asked when he had calmed down a bit.

'That's right. Weird, isn't it?'

'Not so much weird as impossible. I simply don't believe it.'

'Well, that's what Robin said and I've already told you where he got it from.'

'No, no,' he muttered, as though talking to himself. 'Five . . . six hundred possibly, but not more. How could it be more . . . unless . . .'

'Why is it that you find the actual amount so incredible?' I asked him. 'Surely, if you accept the premise that she was blackmailing someone, what difference does it make whether she screwed five hundred out of them or a thousand?'

'Blackmail?' he repeated, looking at me as though he'd forgotten who I was. 'Who said anything about blackmail?'

'How else could she have got hold of a sum like that? And always in cash, don't forget.'

'No, no,' he said, getting up and beginning to walk about on the terrace. 'A double-crosser, perhaps, but not a blackmailer. At least, not in the sense you mean.'

He sat down again, staring in disbelief at his right hand. He had still been clutching his embroidery needle during his peregrination and had somehow contrived to scratch himself. There was a long, thin, pink line near the base of his thumb, red blobs of blood now oozing out of it like tiny blisters. A very minor flesh wound, by the look of it, but he seemed quite shaken and I offered to fetch some disinfectant.

He replied that this might be best, which I interpreted as snatching the chance to compose himself, so that when I returned the mask would be up again and we should hear no more talk of blackmail or double-crossers.

I was wrong, however, because while I was dabbing away at the silly little scratch, he said:

'I think I ought to explain, Tessa.'

'Oh yes?'

'Because something tells me that I could be in a little trouble, if I don't watch out. Tell me, dearest, you who know so much about the seamy side of life: now that the police have caught on to this bank account, am I right in presuming that they will plug away, hell for leather, until they find out where the money came from?'

'I am sure they will try to do so.'

'And would it be equally safe to assume that, if and when they do find out, they will regard themselves as half way towards nabbing the murderer?'

'A little more than half way, I should imagine.'

He sighed: 'I was afraid of that. They'll be wrong, of course, but I see breakers ahead.'

'Why's that, Jamie? Do you know, or can you guess where she got the money from, by any chance?'

'Certainly I know, since it was I who gave it to her.'

137

'For God's sake! You gave Melanie over a thousand pounds? Whatever for?'

'No, not nearly so much; that is what I find so disturbing. I gave her five hundred and, even if you add the fifty she cheated Elfrieda out of, she must still have been very lucky with her investments to have doubled the capital in a few weeks.'

'But why did you give her five hundred pounds?'

'For the most practical of all reasons, to buy her off. Please remember that I'm telling you this in strictest confidence and much against my will. I had hoped it would never come out, but since the chances of that now seem rather frail, I need advice and, so far as I can see, you are the only one who can give it to me.'

'Very well, I'll do my best to remember all that, and I begin to see the light. You gave her the money as a bribe not to gum up your play by appearing in it?'

'Correct! The full stalemate had been reached. Elfrieda was as obstinate as a mule and so, when it's something I care about, am I. It had got to the point where we were barely on speaking terms, which made things very unhappy for both of us, but I could tell that she didn't mean to budge. Then . . . oh, I forget really how it happened, but we were talking here one evening, Viola and I, and it suddenly came to me how stupid and blind we were all being to go on hoping for the impossible, in other words, for Elfrieda to climb down, when all the time it was Melanie we should have been working on.'

I could guess how and from whom this neat suggestion had arrived, but did not interrupt and he went on:

'So I simply offered her five hundred pounds to give herself a little holiday, with the proviso of course that it should be a secret between the two of us, and there we were! All our troubles over. At least, it seemed so at the time.'

'And she took it just like that?'

'As well she might! It was far above equity rates for beginners.'

'I mean, she didn't show surprise or resentment that it should be worth so much to you not to have her in the play?'

'Oh, I believe there was some mild pretence of that kind. How disappointing to have to throw up the part and so forth, but she was willing to make the big sacrifice because she was saving up to get married.'

'Was she really? That's odd!'

'You think so? Personally, I found it rather neat. It enabled us to part on amicable terms, both feeling we'd done the decent thing. She had a certain style, that girl.'

'Was the money all in one lump, or did you dole it out in instalments?'

'No, of course not. Why should I do that when my sole object was to persuade her to shake off the dust of Dearehaven as fast as possible? I handed it over and fervently hoped never to set eyes on her again.'

'Cash or cheque?'

'Open cheque, made out to bearer. That's what worries me so much. That, plus the fact that she seems to have had so much more than I gave her. You don't think she could have altered the amount and forged my initials, by any chance?'

'No, for one thing, your balance would be so much less than it ought to be.'

'It is always so much less than it ought to be,' he admitted sadly. 'Or rather, the overdraft is always so much more.'

'That's very true,' I agreed, 'but, in any case, she could never have got away with a trick like that. At the very least, the bank would have telephoned you before they cashed it.'

'Well, that's some comfort, I suppose. So what do you suggest I do? Sit tight and hope for the best?'

'No, I think that might be fatal. I don't know what becomes of cancelled cheques, but even if they're destroyed immediately, the hunt is on now and, sooner or later, the police are bound to turn up a cashier who remembers all about it. In my opinion, your best bet would be to confess all, before they drag it out of you. The whole truth and nothing but.'

'And will they believe it? Won't they instantly accuse me of having enticed her up here, loaded her with whisky and then pushed her over the cliff?'

'Even if the thought did flit through their heads, there are plenty of people to back up your story. In fact, most of them would frankly admit that, if they'd had five hundred pounds to give away, that's who they'd have given it to, and for exactly the same purpose.'

'Very well, I asked for your advice and I shall follow it. I'm a great believer in that. And so now kindly forget every word I've said, will you?'

'Okay, but before we close the subject for ever, there's just one question I must ask.'

'What's that?' he asked, frowning impatiently.

'It's about that famous occasion when you saw Melanie walking along the top of the cliff, when everyone thought she'd gone for good. Didn't it worry you?'

'Just a little,' he replied, as smoothly as though he had rehearsed the answer. 'Not so badly as you might suppose. You'll remember that I was not absolutely certain that it was her and it was easy to tell myself that I was getting obsessive, seeing Melanie popping up from behind every gorse bush. It wasn't until you arrived from London and told us she'd been on the local train that I became really anxious. After all, I only had her word for it that she would go away and leave us in peace. I had absolutely no

140

way of holding her to it. Fortunately, that gloomy mood didn't last long.'

'Oh, why was that?'

'Don't you remember, darling? It was only twenty-four hours later that poor Elfrieda was gathered. Broken up as I was, as we all were, I could not fail to realise that none of us any longer had anything to fear from Melanie. She had become as powerless as if she had dropped dead from a heart attack herself.'

'Yes, that's true,' I admitted. 'And looking back on it now, quite dispassionately, do you believe it was her you saw?'

'Probably, but I really can't see that it matters any more.'

'What about the young man, though? That could be important. Have you had second thoughts about him, or are you still sure he was a total stranger?'

'Absolutely dead positive,' he replied.

So perhaps, after all, he had been right to disclaim any great acting talent. He had answered without hesitation and the tone perfectly matched the words, but he had been unable to conceal the fleeting, guarded expression in his eyes and I felt absolutely dead positive that he was lying.

EIGHTEEN

The invitation card was large, heavily engraved and carried some rather strange wording. It stated that on 10th June, Mrs Denis Atterbury would be at home at the Royal Metropolitan Hotel, so she must have been a woman in a million. However, the information was at least technically correct because the hotel address was also given for the R.S.V.P. Two other curious features were the handwritten words, 'Mr and Mrs Crichton' in the top left hand corner and a pair of be-ribboned wedding bells in the opposite one.

'I can't go,' Viola said, having presented me with this document on her return from the theatre. 'The 10th is next Saturday and I've got a matinée, as well as the evening show.'

'It looks as though you'll be missing one to knock spots off them both. Who is this woman? She can't be anyone I know?'

'No, but you've met her daughter. She's the one called Marcia and she's going to marry Charlie Henshaw.'

'Oh, I see! Hence the wedding bells! You mean this is an invitation to the reception?'

'Not exactly. The final knot won't be tied for another three weeks. It's what you might call a pre-wedding reception. I've had it all laboriously explained to me by Roger Padmore and you're not expected to send a present or anything.'

'What's the idea then? Just making doubly sure the bridegroom doesn't cut and run?'

Viola looked rather startled: 'You certainly do have a penetrating eye, don't you, Tessa? If you ever give up the stage, I think you should try your hand as a gossip columnist.'

'Thank you. And what would my column be about today?'

'Oh, nothing sensational; only old Padmore did drop a few heavy hints that things have been a bit on-again-off-again with that young couple. However, the reason for the party is much more mundane, you'll be disappointed to hear. These Atterburys live miles away in the industrial north and that's where the wedding will be. Obviously, lots of Charlie's local friends won't be able to get up there for it, so, money being no object, the Atterburys have installed themselves at the hotel for a week, to lay on a party specially for them.'

'Couldn't the Henshaws have done that? They have bags of room at the wee cottage.'

'Perhaps they would have, if Douglas's inheritance hadn't turned out to be so flimsy.'

'You think he might be a bit pushed?'

'Oh, Lord no, not by our standards. Although there did seem to be something phoney in all that ostentation. One had the feeling that it was slightly unreal.'

'Yes, one did.'

'Well, don't quote me, for God's sake,' Viola said. 'It's no concern of ours. Will you go to the party?'

'You bet; but I must try and find somebody to tag along with. I don't want to be all on my own, out in the cold, among the *jeunesse dorée* of Dearehaven.'

The so-called Mr Crichton being unable or unwilling to spare the time to attend this gala, I next tried Len, knowing that he had been invited, but he was almost as unco-operative. He informed me in harassed, yet sanctimonious tones, that with the last full week of rehearsals approaching, he had a lot on his plate just now and, in any case, considered cocktail parties a complete waste of time. He would try to look in for a few minutes at some point during the evening, but I was not to count on him.

Jamie was a washout too. He made no secret of having accepted the invitation, but did not suggest that we should make our entrance together, so I concluded that he had bigger fish to fry. Since every card holder at the Rotunda was in a similar situation to Viola's, and either tied up with performances or else going home for the weekend, I was faced with the choice of staying away or going on my own, and it was the work of a second to decide which.

By seven o'clock on Saturday evening there must have been at least a hundred people congregated in the ballroom of the Royal Metropolitan, but since it could easily have accommodated twice that number without any strain at all, the atmosphere was muted, rather than festive.

A middle-aged couple, obviously Marcia's parents, were standing just inside the entrance with Kitty Henshaw, who looked cross and bored, which was her natural expression, but Douglas was not in evidence. I assumed that either his ankle had not mended sufficiently for him to undertake reception duty, or else that he was busily getting the circulation back into it by chasing round after all the prettiest girls in the room.

I apologised to Kitty for Robin's absence, but, as she once again showed no sign of having the least idea of who I was talking about, this did not get us very far. After a moment's awkward silence, she rallied slightly and said that, since I was on my own, she would introduce me to the best man, who would see that I had a good time.

'He's somewhere about,' she said vaguely. 'Oh yes, over there! Just come here a moment, would you, Simon? Someone I want you to meet.'

The young man she had addressed in this peremptory fashion glanced round warily, then broke into beaming smiles and came over at the gallop. His name was indeed Simon, which broke Kitty's previous track record, but the most extraordinary part of all was that we were not only related in a remote and roundabout way, but our first meeting had also resulted from his being best man at a wedding. This was when his elder brother married Toby's only and beloved daughter, Ellen. I had seen very little of Simon during the intervening two or three years because nowadays he lived mainly in Switzerland, only returning to his native land for a few weeks in the summer. He proudly proclaimed himself to be a tax exile, but to the best of my knowledge had never earned a penny in his life and lived on a handsome allowance from his father; and Ellen had told me that the sad truth was that, having only about half a lung left to function on, he was obliged to spend the greater part of his life breathing up an air so bracing that it did most of the work for him.

He had changed very little since our last meeting, still small, pale and compact looking, with red gold hair puffed up like a halo, and life among the foreigners had not affected his special brand of conversation. When we had both exclaimed over the amazing coincidence of it all, he told me how delighted he was to see me, adding:

'I still love you from afar, you know. Moon about most of the day composing poems in which you are compared rather favourably to the edelweiss and what not; but you know all about that.'

'Always nice to hear it again, but do tell me, Simon, how do you come to be a friend of Charlie Henshaw?'

'We were at school together.'

'There now!'

'Well yes, I recognise that sceptical tone and I can hear you telling yourself that the same thing would apply to approximately nine hundred and fifty men of my age, but the special bond which has kept Charlie and me together all these years is that we were both expelled during the same week.'

'Honestly?'

'Well no, not entirely,' he admitted sadly, 'I am afraid I was boasting a bit there. Getting expelled was the done thing in our day, but I have to confess that with me it was a case of influenza or something. It wouldn't seem to go away and eventually it was decided that I might be better off in some establishment where the water didn't actually freeze overnight in the tooth mugs.'

'And Charlie?'

'Oh, his was a real, *bona fide* expulsion. Nothing bogus about that.'

'What did he do? Or shouldn't one ask?'

'Certainly, one should. We were all very proud of him and still are. He was caught *in flagrante delicto* with the housemaster's niece, who had come there to recuperate from a vicious attack of chicken pox. Quite romantic, really.'

'And how about Marcia? Do you love her from afar, too?'

'I may grow to. I'm working on it.'

'What's the trouble? Don't you find her attractive?'

'Yes, madly. I'm terribly susceptible to goggle eyes and big teeth. She makes me feel like Little Red Riding Hood. The snag is that I prefer the object of my unrequited passion to be unobtainable. It's the key factor.'

146

'So what are you worrying about? There can be few less attainable girls than one who is within three weeks of marrying someone else.'

'Oh, I agree and when the three weeks are up and we all stand side by side at the altar, I shall throw myself into it with might and main, never fear! What makes me hold back is the fear that even at this stage she might return the ring and start asking the real Mr Right to stand up. That could be a worry.'

'Why should she do that? Have there been indications that she is about to transfer her affections?'

'No, it's not as bad as that, but shall I let you into a little secret, Tessa? Yes, I think I will. I know how you love them and perhaps you will be able to laugh away my fears.'

'I'll try my best.'

'I have a nasty feeling it is Charlie who has given his heart to another.'

'Indeed? What makes you think so?'

'I ran across him in London not long ago. That's how he knew I was over here. It was in one of those restaurants in Jermyn Street. I went there with my parents and there was Charlie, lunching with a very sexy number indeed. At any rate, he evidently found her so. I don't know whether you've ever tried to eat your *filet mignon* while sitting opposite a man who is devouring you with his eyes, but if so you'll know what I'm talking about. Anyway, when he telephoned a few days later and requested me to be best man at his wedding, I was not so terribly bowled over.'

'The bowling over part was the discovery that Marcia was not the girl he'd been devouring in the restaurant?'

Just so! Can the marriage last, one asks oneself? Can one even be certain that it will begin?'

147

'Oh yes, I think one can,' I assured him. 'I happen to know quite a lot about these Henshaws and I can tell you that this kind of thing runs in the family. Charlie's father is a great devourer, practically insatiable, I shouldn't wonder, but his marriage has survived in spite of it and here they are, thirty years on and still together.'

'How do you account for it? Her ladyship doesn't strike one as a particularly shrinking violet; not one who would hesitate to scream the roof off if anything displeased her.'

'No, and something tells me that Marcia wouldn't either, but perhaps what they also have in common is the capacity to buckle down to the job, so long as the money's right.'

'Ah yes, but that only raises another snag, I fear. When we were in this restaurant, you see, and I had explained to my parents about Charlie, my dear old dad, who, as you'll no doubt remember, is fairly well informed on the seamy side of commercial life, was telling me that . . .'

'Oh, so here you are at last!' a curt voice said at my elbow. 'I managed to look in, after all, and I've been wondering where you'd got to.'

It was Len and, to add to my annoyance, I saw that his hair was brushed down flat and that he was nattily attired in a dark suit and tie. So he had not only torn himself away from the piled up plate to come to the party, but had obviously put in at least half an hour dolling himself up for it.

It spelt the end of my *tête-à-tête* with Simon, of course, and he soon drifted away, saying that now was the time for all best men to chat up a bridesmaid or two, and the worst of it was that the most important question of all had been left unanswered.

Having successfully gummed up these works, Len proceeded to unendear himself still further by looking round the room and announcing disgustedly:

148

'God, what a collection of over-fed, over-dressed morons! Could anything be more vulgar?'

The fact that my own initial reaction, although less violent, had been somewhat similar for some reason only increased my irritation and I said:

'How can you call them moronic when you don't even know them?'

'I don't want to know them and I don't intend to. I can tell at a glance that they don't speak the same language. They represent every rotten thing in our society that I despise.'

'Rather masochistic of you to come then. You might have guessed what you'd be in for.'

'It's seeing them *en masse* like this which I find so depressing. It would take a hell of a lot of new brooms to sweep this lot away. Shall we go now, or are you enjoying yourself?'

'No, not particularly, but you've only just arrived.'

'On the contrary, I've been here for at least ten minutes, most of it spent looking for you. Still, I'll put up with it for a bit longer, if this is your idea of fun.'

Since he had a car outside and I hadn't, it was not for me to tell him to go and boil himself, but my inner resentment was not appeased by his continuing to lecture me on the decadence of the wealthy middle classes all the way to Viola's house.

I should have realised, I suppose, that such an outburst sprang from a much deeper unhappiness than could have been aroused by the sight of a lot of provincial people wearing their best clothes, but by the time we drew up at the gate I had reached such a pitch of annoyance that I decided to retaliate:

'By the way, Len,' I asked him, 'is it true what they tell me, that you and Melanie had been planning to get married?'

To my horror, the tears started to his eyes and his face turned scarlet. Then, instead of answering, he folded his arms over the steering wheel, lowered his head on to them and started to sob.

I had never felt more miserable or ashamed in my life.

NINETEEN

'I can't tell you what I meant by it,' I confessed to Viola the next morning. 'It was a shocking way to behave. Not only to have dealt such a mean blow at Len, but also in breaking my word to you and Kyril. My only excuse is that he'd been so patronising and priggish ever since he turned up at the party that I finally lost all control. That's why I've told you about it. I knew it would haunt me unless I got it out of my system.'

'Now, listen to me for a minute, please!' Viola said, carefully replacing her coffee cup on its saucer, 'because for once in my life I am going to read the riot act.'

Her governessy tone was just the antidote to remorse I needed and, with a touch of defiance, I said:

'Well, before you begin, I'd just like to point out that disgraceful I may have been, but there must be some truth in what I said, otherwise he wouldn't have gone to pieces like that.'

'That is the crux of what I am about to explain. Personally, I can see now that we were foolish not to put you in the picture as soon as you arrived, but by then all the signs were that Melanie had vanished for good and we could hardly have foreseen that only a few days later she would turn up dead, not a hundred yards from where we're sitting, still less that you would be the one to find her.'

'Forgive me, Viola, but I don't understand you. Surely, her turning up dead on the beach is the only part of the picture that matters. What else could you have told me which had any significance compared to that?'

'And that's another thing. None of us realised what a right little terrier had arrived in our midst; how you'd go ferreting around all over the place, digging out information which would have been better left buried and rabbiting on about your theories to anyone who would listen.'

'Not only a terrier,' I thought to myself, 'a whole blinking menagerie.'

'Don't misunderstand me,' Viola went on. 'There was no sinister conspiracy or anything approaching it; simply a tacit agreement on all our parts. You, after all, were a complete outsider, in that sense, and by the time you joined us the whole tiresome episode appeared to be over. What point would there have been in dragging it all out again? I can see now how mistaken we were, though. If we'd taken you into our confidence and explained things, you might now be working for us, instead of against.'

'I'm not working against you, I resent that. And, even if I were, it wouldn't make any difference. You can't hush up a murder.'

'I realise that. I'm not a complete ostrich, Tessa, but you can avoid bringing suspicion on your own camp.'

'Have I done that?'

'No, not really, I was exaggerating, but that charming little scene between you and Len last night is typical of what I mean. You keep trying to strengthen the links between us and Melanie and it could be so dangerous.'

'So you're implying that there was not only truth in what I said, but that the rest of you have known it all along and are terrified that if the police get to hear about it they will arrest Len on the spot? I don't follow your reasoning. People don't normally go about clobbering other people to death just because they're in love with them.'

Viola shook her head reprovingly:

'You know damn well that it's far more complicated than that. No man-woman relationship could ever be quite straightforward with Len. Emotionally, he's a bagful of contradictions and in this particular affair there were all sorts of additional undercurrents to pull him in different directions.'

'Such as?'

'Jamie's attitude, for one. Why do you imagine he was so shattered by the news that Melanie was to be offered the part of the schoolgirl?'

'For the reason he gave, presumably. That she'd had no experience and would be quite unsuitable. I don't altogether agree with him, but that's beside the point.'

'Oh, come on, Tessa, you're not even trying! Elfrieda may have lost some of her judgement, where Melanie was concerned, but the theatre always came first with her and the theatre, in this context, meant Jamie and his new play. In the normal way, the two of them would have sorted out a disagreement of that kind in no time at all.'

'So what stopped them?'

'Obviously, he refused even to discuss it, putting the onus firmly on Len to keep Melanie out of the cast because what really frightened him was that it probably wasn't Elfrieda, all by herself, who had dreamt up this idea, but that Len, his own protégé, had put it into her head and was actively encouraging her to stick to it.'

'Oh, I see! And you think that if this were brought into the open the police might begin to regard it as some kind of quirky, three-cornered *crime passionelle*? I doubt if there'd be much danger of that, you know. Something tells me that the Dearehaven constabulary are not accustomed to reasoning quite on those lines.'

'I wouldn't bank on it, but the real point is that we don't want them to start asking awkward questions. They might even get the urge to probe a little deeper into Jamie's story of the couple he saw walking on the cliffs. How he must now regret ever having mentioned that! In fact, I think he probably regretted it the moment it was out, which is perhaps why he then . . .'

'Was unable to give any description at all of the young man, except that he was fair haired and wearing jeans, which could apply to several million people and might or might not have been true? Looking back on it, it did strike me as odd, I must confess. He has such a gimlet eye for human idiosyncracies that it was strange that he had not picked out a single feature; narrow shoulders or rolling walk, or something on those lines. So what you're hinting is that he'd recognised Len and then deliberately set about misleading us, realising rather late in the day that there was a stranger in our midst, in the person of myself?'

'I daresay that's the answer, although perhaps I'm only making matters worse by admitting it. Can one assume that you will now go trotting off to the police station and repeat every word?'

'Don't worry,' I told her. 'If Robin had been in charge, there might have been some danger of that, but, as it is, your secret is safe.'

Not that there was any big secret about it, anyway, I could have added, for she was a great weigher up of pros and cons in her lifelong fight to ward off unpleasantness and I felt sure that these so-called indiscretions had been carefully self-edited. She had told me just enough to draw me into the gang, with the consequent obligation of loyalty to its other members, but probably not half of what she knew or suspected. So I tried a last throw:

154

'By the way, Viola; you know all that money Melanie had stashed away in Jill's name? She didn't get any of it from you, did she?'

'From me? Certainly not. What on earth gave you that idea?'

'I thought you might have tried to buy her off. You know, peace at any price?'

'So I might, if I'd thought of it. Not that I could really have afforded to in these hard times, which may be just as well, as things have turned out.'

She made these observations in a thoughtful, rather amused voice and, unfortunately, she was a much better, or at any rate more experienced, actor than Jamie, so I was still no further forward.

TWENTY

'Have you recovered from the shock yet, Jill?' I asked her, carrying my bread and cheese and glass of cider over to the scrubbed wooden bench and table, where she was eating an egg salad, which looked sadly inadequate for her large bony frame.

The custom of lunching in Elfrieda's office had naturally been discontinued after her death and most of us had gravitated to a small and ancient pub by the harbour. It was not popular with the holiday makers, having no garden, no juke box and no carpet on the floor and, although patronised by the fishing community in the evenings, was relatively empty at lunch time.

'Shock?' she repeated in her growly, defensive voice.

'Of being told that everything you said would be taken down and used in evidence?'

'Oh, that! Yes, quite recovered, thanks. They were fairly decent about it when they realised I was the innocent party.'

'I wonder how she got hold of your driving licence?'

'Nothing easier,' Jill replied, pointing to a shabby brown leather bag on a nearby table and I saw what she meant. It must have been months since she had cleared it out and it was so stuffed with papers and possessions that several of the compartments were gaping open.

'I leave it around all over the place too,' she added. 'I suppose I can count myself lucky that she didn't pinch my cheque book and credit card as well.'

'Somehow I don't see her doing that, or even being tempted to. I've learnt a lot about Melanie during these last few weeks and I'm coming to the conclusion that although hers may have been a curious kind of morality, she had her code, all the same. She took things which were absolutely essential to her, but nothing over or beyond.'

'Isn't that what they call splitting hairs?'

'Well, for instance, she put your driving licence back, didn't she?'

'When she had no further use for it.'

'Yes, but it would have been simpler to have chucked it in the harbour, or a public litter bin; and there must have been as much risk in putting it back as in taking it out. And I've always believed there was an even chance that Elfrieda was telling the truth when she said the petty cash cheque was never presented. Everyone assumed that she was covering up for her darling girl, but, after all, Elfrieda had very high principles and I doubt if she'd have condoned a thing like that. Besides, since the darling girl had walked out, there was really no more point in covering up for her. It wouldn't alter the fact that Melanie had taken all she wanted and moved on to a more amusing scene. That must have been the real blow, but I can see that, even when she was reeling under it, her sense of fair play would balk at Melanie being condemned for the one crime she hadn't committed. Oh dear, I do wish she was still alive. There are so many questions I'd like to ask her.'

'Who? Elfrieda or Melanie?'

'Both. Still, no use wasting regrets over that.'

'Quite so, although there's one thing I can tell you which

157

you'd never have heard from Elfrieda if she'd lived to be ninety. Melanie was murdered in her turn, but it was no more than she deserved. In her own sweet fashion she'd already killed Elfrieda.'

'Jill! What are you saying? How do you know?'

'No need to get excited. She was probably miles away when it happened, but I still hold her responsible and I always shall. No amount of sentimental whitewashing on your part will change that, because you don't know the half of it.'

'The half of what?'

'How Melanie used Elfrieda for her own selfish ends, got her all steamed up and jumping about, when she should have been resting and conserving what energy she had left to her. I daresay no one else has told you this. Perhaps they thought there'd be no sense in dragging it all out again, or perhaps they only cared about the things which affected them personally. I don't claim to be any more caring or observant, but it was thrust under my nose. I was always being called in to help arrange things.'

'What kind of things?'

'Well, for instance, when they were going to see a film, which they did about three evenings a week, I sometimes had to telephone the cinema in advance and make sure they had proper facilities for the wheelchair. So there she'd be, poor old love, dragged off to sit through some awful noisy rubbish, when she ought to have been resting in bed, and all because dear little Melanie got so bored whenever she had to spend an evening at home.'

'What else did they do, when they'd worked through all the films?'

'It makes me sick to think of it. Melanie was supposed to be crazy about acting, you know. Showing off was what she was really crazy about. She was forever rigging up silly theatricals for Elfrieda's benefit. She even used to take things home from the wardrobe, borrowing she called it. One evening when Elfrieda got back there was this fool of a girl laid out on the sofa, wrapped in a sheet, with that wet-white stuff all over her face. Honestly, it's a wonder Elfrieda didn't have a heart attack then.'

'Although I suppose the shock can't have been so terrible if she could tell you about it afterwards?'

'She didn't; it was her housekeeper who passed that one on and she did say that after a moment the corpse went into such heaving giggles that no one could have been fooled for long. Long enough for a woman in Elfrieda's condition, though. And then there was the driving; did you hear about that?'

'I knew Elfrieda was paying for her to have lessons.'

'You'd think that would have been enough, wouldn't you? But oh dear, no. She said she'd never get through her test if she didn't have extra practice, so what does Elfrieda do? Only has an L plate stuck on her own car and tells Taylor, her own chauffeur, that he's got to sit in front while Melanie crashes through the gears and stamps her great foot down on the accelerator before she lets the handbrake off.'

'Be fair, Jill! She may have been a very good driver.'

'Not according to Taylor, she wasn't. He was very fed up about what she was doing to his precious car. But Melanie treated the whole thing as a huge joke, didn't care how many scrapes she got into; but that wasn't the worst of it. What really made him angry was the way she insisted on Elfrieda going with them. So there she was, jolting around on the back seat, never knowing from one minute to the next when they were going to knock down a pedestrian or slam into the back of a bus. Hardly the best treatment for an elderly invalid with a dicky heart.'

'Did she complain about it?'

'Never. She'd have sacrificed her life to keep that girl

happy and out of trouble and, if you want my opinion, in the end that's exactly what she did do. And she still had so much good work left to her, if she'd only been left in peace.'

'I'm not arguing about that, Jill. I've learnt enough of what went on to realise that Elfrieda really adored Melanie, but do you honestly believe it was all so one-sided? What you've told me does suggest that, no matter what her original motives may have been, it ended with Melanie growing fond of her in return.'

'Just look out of the window and see if there are any pigs flying around, will you?'

'Why else would she have been so keen to have Elfrieda tagging along on those driving practices?'

'Easy! She had a passion to show off and an audience of one was better than nothing. An audience of two was twice as good.'

'You'd reject the idea that, however misguidedly, she thought it was better for Elfrieda to be out and about and having fun, rather than spending evening after evening in her gloomy old house?'

'Absolutely, and if you imagine Melanie had a single unselfish thought tucked away in that busy little brain of hers, you're a bigger fool than I took you for.'

My mild little counter-attack was making her so flushed with anger that the time had come to drop it and I asked her:

'Since you were unaware that your driving licence had gone. I suppose you are just as ignorant as to when it was returned?'

'It's not hard to guess though, is it? Presumably, she took it on the day she opened the bank account and replaced it at the first opportunity.'

'But you don't know it for a fact?'

'I've said so, and I don't see that it matters.'

'Unless she had some further use for it. Like hiring a car, for instance? That could explain how she managed to vanish so effectively. She could have taken one out for twenty-four hours, paid cash in advance, forged your name on the contract and produced your licence.'

'Aren't you forgetting something?'

'Probably.'

'Such as the little matter of returning the car after the twenty-four hours had expired?'

'No, I hadn't overlooked that, I had assumed that it would have been her accomplice's job. He could have driven it back late at night, left it outside the firm's premises and pushed the keys through their letter box. That's often done and my point is that, although the police have doubtless covered every speck of the ground, so far as public transport is concerned, they haven't necessarily been round to all the car hire firms, to find out whether any of them has rented one recently to a certain Jill Sandford.'

I did not honestly believe that the police would have neglected such an obvious point as this, although my contention that Melanie must have had private transport was perfectly genuine, but the main object was to prolong the conversation with Jill for as long as was feasible. I had reached the stage by then of being certain that I had all the information that was needed to solve Melanie's murder, except the final thread that would bind everything neatly together. Someone, somewhere, I was equally convinced, possessed that thread, without in the least recognising its significance and, although the chances of its being Jill were remote in the extreme, I could not afford to eliminate her entirely. So my object was to keep probing away until her patience ran out, and that this was liable to happen sooner than I would have wished became clear with her next words:

'In that case, why not toddle off to the station now and suggest it to them? I'm sure all contributions, however small, would be gratefully received.'

'It wouldn't be much use unless you could confirm that your licence wasn't returned until, let's say, within two days of her disappearance. I imagine she could have arranged to rent a car that much in advance, though probably not longer. The bigger the gap the greater the risk of being found out.'

It had been a very long shot indeed and hopes of its landing on a target so faint that I was not gravely disappointed when she said:

'Then I'm afraid I'm no help. Unless I'm actually asked to produce it, I don't look at my driving licence from one year's end to the other. Why should I?'

'No reason.'

'Anyway, what's all this about an accomplice?'

'Hadn't you heard? The theory is that she must have had one; someone with no police record, who may not live in Dearehaven and who provided the secret refuge when she disappeared off the face of the map. They don't see how she could have managed it without a little help from someone.'

To my astonishment, Jill laid down her fork and stared at me with great intensity:

'You're not having me on, by any chance, Tessa?'

'Certainly not. I thought everyone knew, by now.'

'And they believe it to be someone who doesn't belong here? A stranger, whom none of us has ever seen?'

'Most likely, which is why the police have no clue to his or her identity.'

'And do they also believe he or she to be the murderer?'

'Also likely.'

'My God, what a relief!'

'Why? Were you afraid it might have been one of us?'

162

'Oh Lord, no. What a ridiculous thing to say: I suppose that's your idea of a joke?'

'On the contrary, never more serious. If you had denied being afraid it was one of us, I should have said you were either lying or mentally subnormal. I am sure that everyone at the Rotunda has been secretly afraid all along that it was one of us.'

'Do you mean that, Tessa? Here I've been thinking what a swine I was even to . . . Oh well, never mind, and of course it's so jolly easy for you, isn't it? When you refer to "one of us" in that breezy way, you don't really include yourself, do you?'

'Which may be why I've been more anxious than you to find out just who was responsible.'

'Meaning that your loyalties lie elsewhere?'

'Not at all. Unlike you, I don't find it easy to believe that anyone at the Rotunda is capable of murder. It doesn't seem to belong with the theatrical temperament. The impulse may be present from time to time, just as much as in other people, but I doubt if it often gets put into practice. In fact, with the exception of Mr Booth and President Lincoln, I can't recall a single case. But it still doesn't prevent everyone feeling uneasy and nervous, which is the worst possible thing for their morale and which affects me just as badly as anyone else. You must have noticed how jumpy they've all become? Even poor Janice goes around with a hunted expression nowadays, as though she imagined everyone suspected her of murdering Melanie to get her part back. As for Len, well, you know what he's like at rehearsals now? We'll all be nervous wrecks if it goes on much longer and, with the first night only a week away, that's not a very happy prospect. In my opinion, it would be far better for everyone to stop covering up, for fear of endangering one of their friends, and to tell the police anything which could possibly be relevant. In that way, they could get on with the real job without both hands tied behind their backs.'

'You seem to have great faith in them, but I suppose that's only natural.'

'They're not all fools, you know, Jill. It's just that very few of them are used to dealing with a hunch like they're up against here. Most of the general public dissolve into blobs of putty when they find themselves at the centre of a murder case, but actors are not only trained and experienced in saying things that aren't true, while they're saying them they actually become true. Oh well, here I go again, jogging around on my hobby horse and I don't suppose I've persuaded you by one jot or tittle, whatever they may be. Come on, let's go, shall we? I expect it's high time we struggled back for another miserable, nerve-stretching session at the theatre.'

Jill picked up the bulging bag, draped her shoulders with the old mud coloured leather coat, which she always wore in fair weather or foul, and followed me out of the pub. I honestly did not believe for a moment that I had converted her, but was not unduly depressed, since I also considered it likely that she was one of the few people who had nothing whatever to conceal.

I was wrong on both counts, however, for only a few hours later, after another enervating and ragged rehearsal session, I was walking through the town on my way to have a drink with Kyril and I saw her dusty, beaten up old Renault parked outside the police station.

It was doubtless as a direct result of this that Inspector Watson called soon after nine on the following morning, to put a few questions to Viola.

TWENTY-ONE

We were both in dressing gowns when he arrived, dawdling over our coffee in her tiny dining room and, since it quickly became apparent that my presence at the interview was not required, I stacked the cups on to a tray and carried it out to the kitchen, leaving the door an inch or two open. To my chagrin, however, two seconds later one of them got up and shut it securely, effectively blocking out all sound from the adjoining room.

Since I had carelessly overlooked the fact that, apart from a high and narrow window, the only way out was by the way I had come in, I was stuck there at their pleasure, a prisoner in solitary confinement. I doubt whether Viola's kitchen had been given such a thorough turn-out since the day she moved in.

'I suppose you heard all that?' she asked, when my release came forty minutes later.

'Most of it,' I replied, being a gambler by nature.

'I seem to have got myself into a bit of a jam, don't I?'

'Yes, you do rather.'

'Do you think he believed my explanation?'

'Hard to say,' I admitted very frankly, adding: 'I

couldn't see his expression, you know, and that often reveals more than words.'

'I don't see why he shouldn't believe me. It was a perfectly reasonable thing to do and I acted entirely on my own initiative. No one else was involved and it wasn't part of a plot. The trouble is that I can't prove that.'

'No, I suppose not.'

'Besides, it's not as though she were killed in my flat, is it? My God, I suppose I ought to be on my knees thanking Him that she wasn't!'

'Yes, I suppose you ought,' I agreed, taking a deep breath to stop myself from fainting with curiosity.

'You've become strangely terse and laconic all of a sudden,' Viola said, eyeing me suspiciously. 'Why is that, I wonder?'

'You sound as though you're whistling in the dark,' I told her. 'I thought I shouldn't interrupt until the melody was finished.'

'It's finished now. The longer I think of it, the clearer it becomes that he was bluffing. I haven't done anything criminal and it certainly had no connection with her murder. How could it have?'

'How indeed? But what exactly was she doing in your flat, Viola? I didn't catch that part?'

'What do you mean, you didn't catch that part?' she asked, jerking her head up. 'That part, as you call it, was the crux and heart of the whole interview. He went on digging away at it for about ten minutes.'

'Oh well, perhaps I had my head in the gas oven at that time. I've been cleaning out your stove.'

'A likely tale, I must say!' Viola said, giving me a very baleful look. 'The truth is that I've jumped straight into your little trap, haven't I? Honestly, you must be about the most deceitful young woman who ever drew breath.

166

You didn't hear a single word that passed between me and the Inspector, did you? Come on now, own up!'

I did so, thinking to myself that if ever I heard a kettle called black, she was the pot who was doing it and adding:

'Obviously, I'd never have got anything out of you unless I pretended to know at least half the story already, and in fact it's not nearly so sensational as you appear to believe. I always guessed that Melanie got away from here by car. The very first move would have been to take her photograph round all the railway and bus stations and she was so distinctive, in personality as well as looks, that it wouldn't have taken long to find out where she went and whether she was travelling alone. So when that failed, it left only one question. Not: did she go by car, but whose car was it? Now that we seem to have got the answer to that one, there's really no need to explain any more. Anyway, I can guess.'

'Is that so? And what is your guess?'

'You were simply putting your own precept into practice. You told me once that the best way to settle the argument between Jamie and Elfrieda would be to persuade Melanie to give up the part voluntarily. So I daresay you had the bright idea of offering her a trip to London, with free board and lodging. What puzzles me, though, is why you've been so secretive about it. I'd have been congratulating myself in loud, clear tones and wasting no time in passing on the news.'

'I'll explain why in a minute, but before we come to that I must tell you that you've got it completely wrong.'

'I have?'

'Completely. This was the second time she disappeared. The argument between Jamie and Elfrieda was already over because Elfrieda was dead. And there was no question of board and lodging either, free or otherwise. She stopped me and asked for a lift up to London and I gave her one. Literally as simple as that.'

'Did she tell you why she wanted to go there?'

'No, and I didn't enquire. I hoped that once she got to the big city she'd get lost in it and Dearehaven would see her no more.'

'So what exactly did happen?'

'I picked her up at the first roundabout on the London road. It was about four-thirty, wasn't it, when I left? I'd meant to get away earlier, but Toby and Robin arrived just as I was leaving and that delayed things a bit.'

'Sorry about that.'

'Oh, not at all, I was delighted to see them; only it does show how some tiny incident like that can lead to the most troublesome consequences. Anyway, when I got to the roundabout there was this girl thumbing a lift. I don't normally stop for them, but when I saw who she was I was only too pleased to help her on her way.'

'Did she have any luggage with her?'

'One of those great big plastic carrier bags, but that doesn't mean anything. All girls of that age seem to lug great big carrier bags with them nowadays, whether they're going out to tea or stopping for a fortnight.'

'So you drove all the way to London together, and what did you talk about? Presumably, you didn't sit side by side for four and a half hours without exchanging a little light conversation now and again?'

'As a matter of fact, it was considerably longer than that. More like six hours. There was a heatwave that weekend, if you remember, and we got terribly held up in traffic jams, but the worst thing of all was that we'd only gone about five miles when I had a puncture.'

'That was bad luck. What did you do?'

'Cursed and swore for a bit, naturally. Then I thought of getting to a telephone and asking you to find a garage who could send someone out, but of course that wouldn't have been any use because you'd gone to The Green Man by then. In the end it was Melanie who solved the problem.'

'By changing the wheel?'

'Good God, no, I can't see her doing that, can you? No, she told me to keep out of sight while she flagged down a car, and I must say it worked like a charm. Two stalwart lads appeared on the scene in no time at all. I think they were a little disappointed to discover that she had a chaperone, but they did the job very efficiently.'

'Yes, it's curious about Melanie. She could charm certain birds off the trees whenever she felt like it. However, go on! What did you talk about for six hours?'

'Nothing much. I'd been rather dreading that part of it, because I found her conversation pretty trying at the best of times, but as it happened I got off lightly. She slept for most of the way and the rest of the time she kept herself occupied by twiddling about with the radio knobs to find some pop music. That was maddening enough, God knows, but better than having to listen to her tedious prattle.'

'So you never found out one single thing about where she'd been or where she was heading for?'

'Oh yes, one or two stray bits emerged. She told me that she was planning to spend the weekend in London, but that she wouldn't need a lift back, thanks very much, and not that she'd been offered one, I might add, because she wasn't sure when she'd be leaving and she'd hitch her way back. That sounded promising, because either she didn't intend to return at all, or at the very least she didn't want to commit herself. The idea of thumbing a lift was reasonable too. The railway fare is quite steep, as you know, and that was before we heard about all that money she had stashed away in Jill's name.'

'Although we did know that she'd just inherited ten thousand pounds.'

Viola looked startled: 'Yes, you're right. How extraordinary, I'd forgotten all about that, and she didn't mention it either. Oh well, that's quite understandable, of course; Mr Padmore had no means of getting in touch with her, had he?'

'Did you discover where she was staying in London?'

'No. When we got to the Chiswick flyover I told her I'd be turning off at the next exit and asked if she wanted to be dropped at a tube station. She said that, as she still had to get across to the other side of London, she'd like to clean up a bit and would I mind awfully if she came with me to the flat? I was a bit annoyed because all I wanted was to get home and have a hot bath and go to bed, but I could hardly tell her to go and look for a public lavatory at that time of night.'

'So you did the decent thing and took her home with you? How long was she there?'

'Nearly half an hour, twenty minutes of which she spent in the bathroom, for which I could cheerfully have killed her. When she came out she'd got a brand new hair style and about half a pound of make-up on her face. Elfrieda would have had a fit, but I have to admit that she looked quite attractive, in a tarty sort of way.'

'And what happened during the rest of the time? The ten minutes when she wasn't in the bathroom?'

'She asked if she could use the telephone. She said she'd only just realised how late it was and she wanted to ring her friend where she was staying and make sure there'd be somebody there to let her in. I told her to go ahead.'

'Ah! So perhaps we're getting somewhere at last. Did her friend answer?'

'Apparently.'

'And could you glean anything about him or her from the conversation?'

'Nothing whatever, as you'd have heard me telling the Inspector, if you'd really been able to listen in. I was in quite a hurry to get to the bathroom myself by that time and I left her to it. All I can tell you is that she must have known the number by heart. She didn't look it up or check in her diary, just plonked herself down on the floor and started to dial.'

'Which suggests that she expected it to be a longish call. Was she still at it when you came out of the bathroom?'

'No, the telephone was still on the floor, needless to say, but the bird had flown: carrier bag and all.'

'What, just like that? With no word of farewell?'

'Just one word, as it happens: "Thanks", scrawled in lipstick on my most cherished mirror. Silly little fool! It took me ages to get all the smudges off.'

'And that was the last you saw of her?'

'The very last and you can probably see why I kept quiet about the whole episode? I was hoping she'd gone for good this time and then, of course, when we heard she'd been murdered I didn't dare speak up. I just kept my fingers crossed and hoped it would never come out. Unfortunately, though, this flair of hers for causing trouble seems to be just as active now she's dead as when she was alive. Somebody must have seen her leaving my flat and eventually reported it to the police. They wouldn't tell me who it was though.'

'Probably because no such person exists. I don't believe in that explanation for one minute.'

'What other could there be?'

'Well, look, Viola, it's now nearly three weeks since she was killed. People have stopped talking about it and they don't even show her face on television any more. So why should anyone have waited all this time before going to the police? Either they'd have acted straight away, or not at all.'

'Not necessarily; not, for instance, if they were the timid sort, who dreaded getting mixed up with the police. They might have hung back until the last possible moment, trusting to luck that the case would be solved without their intervention and only feeling compelled to come forward when it became evident that this wasn't going to happen. I repeat: how else could the police have got to hear about it?'

'I don't suppose they did get to hear about it. You accused me of laying a trap for you, but the fact is that you'd already fallen into a much bigger one.'

'How did I? What are you talking about?'

'It's one of the oldest tricks in the trade and in the present case it would have worked something like this: someone here in Dearehaven, who knows you and also knew Melanie, saw you stop at the roundabout and take her on board. Not a distant acquaintance either, but somebody who knew enough to be aware that you were on your way to London. So when the long conflict between conscience and loyalty had at last been resolved, this someone passes on the information to the police, who naturally assume there's a fair chance you drove Melanie the whole way. Better than fair, in fact, since you have not seen fit to mention the incident yourself. However, they also realise that if they were to say to you: "And what happened after you picked her up at the roundabout?", quick as a flash the answer would come that you'd dropped her off at the nearest bus stop, waved goodbye and never saw her again. Isn't that so?'

'Possibly.'

'And they, of course, would have no way of proving that it wasn't true. Whereas, by bluffing you into the belief that they knew it all, you would doubtless say to yourself that it would be pointless, possibly dangerous to deny it.'

'Yes, yes, but listen, Tessa, this makes no sense whatever. When you speak of someone who knew me by sight, I suppose that could apply to any number of people, including a lot of theatre-goers, but to have recognised Melanie as well and to have guessed I was on my way to London, well, that narrows the field considerably.'

'Yes, it does.'

'In other words, what you're implying is that it was someone from the Rotunda?'

'Yes, I am.'

'Then you're barking up completely the wrong tree. That is the most ridiculous suggestion.'

'Why?'

'I doubt if I could explain it in a way you'd understand. You arrived too late on the scene to feel its influence, but there was a tradition of loyalty and comradeship which was quite unique. It was one of the things which made it so lovely to work there. No jealousies or backbiting, just everyone pulling together for the general good. It was something we all recognised and shared and I don't believe it could ever be entirely lost. Certainly, there's enough of it left to make your suggestion completely and utterly out of the question.'

It would have been useless to argue with her. People mainly believe what they need to believe and it is destructive, as well as time-wasting, to try and shake them out of it. Moreover, the only witness I could have called in my defence was Jill and I had no wish to betray her, or the fact that her car had been parked outside the police station the previous evening. So, pretending to be won over, I said:

'Then I am to take it that it is quite beyond the bounds of possibility that someone from the Rotunda saw Melanie get into your car and later reported the fact? That it was some snooper in London who did the damage?'

'It must have been. It was a chance in a million, in a big anonymous block like mine, where half the tenants wouldn't recognise their next door neighbours if they passed them in the street, but all the same it has to be the answer.'

She sounded so positive about it that for a couple of seconds I was almost tempted to believe her.

TWENTY-TWO

My task, like Jamie's, was now almost finished and, to continue with the simile, only one or two more stitches were needed to fill in the background. For one of them I needed the observant eye of Simon.

It took me the best part of a day to track him down because my telephone call to his parents' home in London by a great mischance was answered by his mother, who was most unwilling to part with any information concerning his whereabouts until I had disclosed my identity. I was equally reluctant to comply with this condition, because I knew this jealous, possessive mother of old and if by any chance Simon had burbled on to her in his merry fashion about loving me from afar, I knew that afar was where she would wish it to remain and would go to any lengths to put me off his track.

Having drawn a blank there, I next appealed to my cousin Ellen. She was no help either, but promised to ask Jeremy as soon as he came in and, faithful and true as ever, reported back at six-thirty that evening with an address and telephone number in Sussex.

Luckily, I was alone at the cottage at the time, Viola being still at the theatre and, as yet, no Jamie plying his needle on the terrace. So I immediately seized the telephone again and, with only a little more delay, was at last connected with my quarry.

'Sweet of you to say so, Simon,' I told him, interrupting the compliments with a rush of sibilants, 'but I only have a few minutes and there's something important I want to ask you.'

'Ask away, dear heart! Answering your questions is one of life's least onerous tasks.'

'Do you remember telling me, when we met at the party, how you'd seen your friend, Charlie, lunching in a restaurant in London?'

'Yes, clearly. Is that the question?'

'No, it's this: can you describe the girl who was with him?'

'Oh well, now, let me see! Very dishy, as I think I mentioned, if you happen to approve of that sort of thing.'

'What sort of thing?'

'Give me a moment to do some total recall and I'll paint you the full picture.'

'No, that won't be necessary and there isn't time; just one feature which struck you particularly will do. Like the colour of her hair, for instance?'

'Oh yes, indeed, that's very easy,' he said and proceeded to describe it to perfection.

Jamie turned up a few minutes after I put the telephone down and when the first of the champagne had done its job in mellowing his mood and bolstering my courage, I told him that I now understood why, when asked if he recognised the young man who had been walking on the cliff with Melanie, his denial the first time had appeared to be true, and the second time untrue.

'Oh, you do, do you?' he enquired, snipping off a few knots.

'All part of the policy of being nice to Douglas, I take it? His then having become the hand which fed us?'

'Dearehaven is having a bad effect on you,' he said. 'You are becoming much too cynical.'

However, he had not denied the charge and it did not appear to have put him out of humour, so I whiled away the rest of the interval until Viola's return by laying a bet with him. This can often be a useful gambit for obtaining information which would otherwise be inaccessible, because when there is money at stake many people, specially those who don't need it, will exert themselves to find the correct answer. In fact, he acted most promptly and was able to give it to me the next morning.

Before all this came about, I had found time to call at the main Dearehaven post office and, after the usual waiting in line and wishing I had joined any other queue except the one I was in, received my reward in the form of an envelope addressed to Mrs R. Price, c/o Poste Restante.

The letter inside was very stilted and genteel and, in any case, it was only one more step in the process of elimination, but it told me everything I needed to know, and I was so glad that I had followed Mrs Bracegirdle's advice.

TWENTY-THREE

The opening night of *Au Pair* was to have been on the following Tuesday, but several days before that the Rotunda had become a forlorn and silent building. The glass cases outside, which had formerly contained photographs of the cast, were now empty, with black and yellow stickers pasted across them, saying CLOSED, and Robin and I were at Roakes Common, spending the weekend with Toby.

'Jill's the one I feel worst about,' I told them. 'I feel bad about all of them, of course, although I suppose it will only be a temporary set-back for Jamie. His play is sure to come into London the minute there's a theatre available, and there are hints that I may come with it; but it's rough on the others being left high and dry in the middle of the season, even if Douglas does do the decent thing by way of compensation.'

'Why is it any worse for Jill?'

'Because I deceived her. Quite inadvertently, I might add, but she's never going to believe that. When I tried to say goodbye yesterday she wouldn't utter a word. Just looked at me as though I was Judas Iscariot, which I am sure is how she feels. The Rotunda wasn't simply a job to her; more like a religion.'

'How do you deceive someone inadvertently?' Toby asked. 'It might be a trick worth knowing.'

'I told her, with my hand on my heart, that no one connected with the theatre could have killed Melanie. She trusted me and that's why she felt safe in going to the police. The ironic part is that I meant it, at the time, although if we'd had our talk only a day or two earlier, I wouldn't have said it because that was before I finally crossed Len off my list of suspects and narrowed it down to two.'

'Which two were they?' Toby asked.

'Henshaw, *père et fils*.'

'And what had poor Len done to get himself on the list?' Robin asked. 'The only time I met him he struck me as a particularly non-violent type.'

'I agree, and it was after my painful scene with him in the car that he was definitely eliminated. Anyone who broke into floods of tears at the mention of a dead girl must have liked her a little too much to have murdered her. In a funny way, I believe he may have loved her for years, though perhaps more as a baby sister than in the conventional sense. The problem was that he'd come out with one or two fair old whoppers and there seemed to be no point or purpose in them, unless he was concealing something so monumentally damaging that he hardly dared to speak the truth about anything, for fear of betraying himself.'

'Though he can't have whoppered very convincingly, by the sound of it?'

'No, and although he was indeed concealing something, the mistake was in assuming that it was connected with Melanie's murder.'

'And what was it connected with?'

'His past.'

'Oh, really? What was so disgraceful about that?'

179

'Nothing. It was a sight too graceful, in fact. He was bitterly ashamed of his bourgeois background and he'd put it around that he came from the slums of Bermondsey or somewhere. So he lived in constant fear of being unmasked as a nicely brought up fake from a prosperous middle class family. You can't altogether blame him. Judging by her letter, his mother must be one of the most prissy and pretentious women alive and even at the age of ten Melanie openly despised her.'

'Whatever are you talking about, Tessa?' Robin asked. 'Since when have you been in correspondence with Len's mother and how does the ten-year-old Melanie come into it?'

'She was pushed into it by the orphanage matron, but I'm getting out of sequence. To revert to Len and his false pretences, the very first time I met him we were driving through the town and he told me that it used to have great charm and character until the vandals got their hands on it, so naturally I asked him if he'd known it in the old days, thinking he might have been taken their for holidays as a child or something. He denied it hotly, as though I'd accused him of something insulting. Then later on I found that he was very knowledgeable about all the local cab firms, although he had his own car and couldn't have had much occasion to use them. The most curious thing of all was that he was able to tell me exactly how to get to the crematorium. That, in my opinion, is in the category which separates the native from the visitor in one stroke. So it was obvious that he had strong associations with Dearehaven, only I still couldn't understand why it was something to be ashamed of. Then I remembered Kyril once telling me that Len's father had been a pharmacist and that made everything perfectly clear.'

'It would, of course,' Toby said. 'I do see that.'

'The word pharmacist,' I explained, 'conjured up rather

impressive visions of a man in a white coat peering at bugs through a microscope and inventing wonder drugs to kill them off; but then I realised that this was just one of Kyril's Gallic affectations and that what he actually meant was a man in a white coat peering at prescriptions in a chemist's shop in the High Street.'

'It gets clearer by the minute.'

'Not to you or Robin, of course, but that's because neither of you overheard my conversation with the Matron of the Brackley Place Children's Home. She told me that one of the families Melanie was sent to for a trial visit were people who owned a chemist's shop in the town. She also threw in the fact that they had a child of their own, who was old enough to go to college. So, if the boy in question was our Len, that would explain a lot of things.'

'One thing it doesn't explain, though,' Robin objected, 'is that if Len remembered her well enough to feel like Big Brother, why didn't Melanie remember him?'

'I feel sure she did, and that when she turned up in his life again, so inopportunely, he begged her not to let on about his shameful origins. She, being a good sport in many ways, cheerfully entered into the spirit of things and in fact never gave him away. No wonder he felt affection and gratitude. Having established this glamorous reputation for grinding his way up from the lowest depths of the working classes, he'd have looked a proper ass if the truth had come out about his college education.'

'Would she really have been so co-operative? I thought she was supposed to be such an unprincipled tramp, who would only have kept quiet about a thing like that in return for money in the bank?'

'No, she wasn't greedy or spiteful, whatever some people have tried to pretend; but the trouble was that she brought out very strong reactions in everyone who met her. Some people hated and feared her almost instinctively, but

181

Elfrieda, who had shown once before that she had a particular weakness for irreverent young people, really loved her. And I don't care what they say, I still believe it was mutual. Another very important thing is that she had enormous sex appeal. Women either didn't recognise it, or detested her even more because of it, but it affected every man to some extent. I daresay that Len's feelings weren't purely platonic and even Jamie admitted that there was something attractive in her coltishness. As for Simon, whom I like to think of as the number one expert in these matters, he described her as a very sexy number indeed.'

'Who is Simon?' Toby asked.

'The brother of your son-in-law. He saw Melanie lunching with Charlie Henshaw in London. But I'll come back to Simon in a moment, because he supplied another piece of information, equally valuable in its way. First, though, there is one more thing you should know about Melanie. She was no paragon and I don't doubt that she nicked a bit here and there, but I question if she was a confirmed thief, still less that she would have stolen from someone who had been good to her. Mrs Bracegirdle had certainly never seen her in that light, and I had a bet with Jamie, who checked it out with Mr Padmore. It was quite true what Elfrieda said about the petty cash cheque, it was never presented.'

'In that case, why offer to take it to the bank?' Robin asked.

'Probably to give herself extra leeway. I'm guessing now, but she may have needed time to get away before the alarm was raised. She'd already put it about that her driving instructor often let the lessons run on a bit and, if she had to call at the bank as well, it would have given her at least a couple of hours' start. She was a naughty girl all right, but not an evil one.'

'And what about all that money she had stashed away

under a false name? You don't pretend she came by that honestly?'

'Oh yes, I do. We know that part of it was a bribe from Jamie and no doubt some had been handed out by Elfrieda, for clothes and so on. The rest was provided by the young man she was in love with. In that sense, it was a joint account. She told several people that she was saving up to get married and it was true. When she first disappeared it was to spend the weekend with him and work out their plans. Why they didn't get married then I'll never know, but perhaps she wanted to tell Elfrieda about it and if possible get her approval before she took the plunge. Anyway, she must have been on her way back to meet him in London again when Viola picked her up at the roundabout and I'm sure she believed she would be a married lady before the week was out.'

'And what about this charming young man? Is he in trouble?'

'Not in the legal sense, because he's done nothing criminal and, as you know, he's going to marry someone else in a week's time. Having met her, I'd say, he was going to be in another sort of trouble, however.'

'How did he and Melanie meet in the first place?'

'Don't you remember? The first place was in his own home, nearly five years ago, when she was fourteen and big for her age, I shouldn't wonder. Charlie was a few years older and Melanie went there for the second of her trial visits. She wasn't particularly welcome, but Elfrieda talked them into it and I suppose Douglas was willing to do her a small favour for old times' sake. Unfortunately, it all turned out disastrously and Melanie was packed off back to Mrs Bracegirdle, ostensibly for stealing, although of course that wasn't the reason at all. I've learnt enough about her, in my researches, to find that sort of ingratitude quite out of character.'

'What was the reason, then?'

'Charlie seduced her, I haven't a doubt of it. He's a chip off the old block and Simon told me that he'd already been expelled from school for the same sort of prank. Presumably, his mother discovered what was going on and had Melanie out of there in a matter of hours. However, she wasn't going to let her darling boy's reputation be smirched, so she trumped up the story of the theft. I don't know whether the baby that was born after she ran away from the Home was Charlie's or not, but it would never surprise me, and I daresay Elfrieda may have had misgivings about it too, which could account for her taking Melanie under her wing in the first place. Furthermore, I wouldn't mind betting that Melanie's main reason for picking on Elfrieda and the Rotunda was in the hope of getting in touch with Charlie, which is exactly what happened, and as soon as they set eyes on each other, it all started up again. He was already engaged to Marcia by then, but Viola told me that it had been broken off for a time and then patched up again.'

'Poor old Viola,' Toby said, sounding genuinely sad about it. 'Couldn't you have let her off? Just this once, I mean? I am sure she would never have done such a thing again.'

Robin looked rather shocked by this and I said:

'I am sure everyone at the Rotunda wanted to ask the same question and I confess that I might have kept out of it, if I had known from the start where it would end. I was led astray partly by Jamie's assertion that Melanie's death coming after Elfrieda's put all of them in the clear. They all had motives of a kind for wanting her out of the way while Elfrieda was alive, but after her death there was absolutely no incentive whatever. She appeared then to be stripped of all her power, but it wasn't entirely true

184

because what Jamie didn't know was that Elfrieda had not died from purely natural causes.'

'So you were right, after all?' Toby said. 'And how restrained of you not to sound smug!'

'Oh, I knew I could depend on you to tell me that I told you so. Besides, just feeling it in my bones didn't get me very far. I was still stuck with the fact that, on the face of it, the last thing any of our lot wanted was for Elfrieda to leave the scene, so at that point Douglas went swooping up to the top of my list. He at least had a nice, straightforward motive: to get his hands on her money before it was all whittled away.'

'And for Melanie?'

'Money once again. To ensure that his son married the rich girl, instead of the poor one. It seemed a fairly satisfactory answer until Viola gave the real game away.'

'How?'

'First by insisting that it was inconceivable that anyone at the Rotunda could have reported to the police that they'd seen Melanie get into her car at the roundabout. She would have it that someone had noticed her leaving the London flat. When I pointed out how unlikely it was that this unknown witness would have waited for almost three weeks, she still refused to consider any alternative and launched into that little sermon about the wonderful Three Musketeers spirit they all had.'

'Which did exist, though, did it not?'

'For many of them, Jill in particular, and Len too; but not quite in the same way for Viola. She'd been around too long to be starry eyed about it. In fact, she must have guessed that as soon as Elfrieda died the good old team spirit would begin to crumble away. So, on the assumption that she was trying to deceive either herself or me, I looked at the question from the other side and immediately got a totally different answer.'

'You are always making cryptic remarks like that,' Toby complained, 'and I am sure it is done to keep us on our toes, though without much success, in my case. What was this question?'

'Can it be,' Robin asked thoughtfully, 'that Melanie never went to her flat at all?'

'Right first go! Every single word she told me about what happened after she stopped at the roundabout was a farrago. She got badly tangled up once or twice, but it wasn't such a bad circumstantial account, considering that she more or less had to make it up as she went along, but she was rotten on details.'

'I didn't notice many lapses in that respect,' Toby said. 'She even told you to the minute how long each of them spent in the bathroom.'

'I know, but she also said that the journey took almost six hours instead of the usual four and a half. That was to bolster up her alibi, of course, but she was careless about it and one reason she gave for the delay was that because of the heatwave there were enormous traffic jams. All nonsense, you know. The heavy traffic would have been on the other carriage way, coming out of London, not going in. And when I asked her what they'd talked about during all that time she couldn't come up with a single topic. She tried to get around that by saying Melanie had spent most of the time asleep, but I ask you? Between five and ten in the evening when, if there was one thing that girl was noted for, it was her tremendous vitality. The truth is that Viola detested her, never bothered to observe or listen to her and so couldn't trust herself to invent any authentic sounding dialogue.'

'And did you find out what really happened after they met at the roundabout?' Robin asked.

'Well, that's the sad and horrifying part about it, because nothing at that point was premeditated. She had no harmful intentions and her simple object was to speed Melanie on her way. However, when they'd driven a few miles it struck her that she'd left something essential behind at the cottage. No doubt, it was the excitement of meeting you two which put it out of her head. Anyway, she remembered and turned back. Still no ulterior motive, you understand, but at some point on this part of the journey Melanie must have said something which turned her heart to stone. Then, when she arrived at the cottage and found our note saying we'd all moved out, I suppose it was like some sort of message from above, exhorting her to take her courage in both hands and deal with Melanie once and for all. So she opened a bottle of Jamie's champagne, laced Melanie's share with a stiff dollop of brandy and, when she'd got her really drunk, coshed her with one of those rocks from the garden. As soon as it was dark enough she pushed her into the car, drove it as near to the edge of the cliff as she dared and shoved her over. After that it was simply a matter of walking down to Rocky Cove and covering the body with all the loose rocks and lumps of chalk she could lay her hands on, before belting off to London. She must have reckoned that weeks could go by before the deed was discovered and so they might have, if it hadn't been for Toby's passion for privacy, and if she hadn't been careless enough to leave that hand uncovered.'

'How do you know all this?' Robin asked. 'Did Viola tell you?'

'Some of it, when she saw the game was up. Most of it I had already guessed, so I was able to tell her.'

'You were taking rather a chance, if I may say so,' Toby remarked. 'If you had guessed wrong, it would have spelt the end of your friendship; although I daresay it will do that, anyway.'

'And, since you appear to have based your case mainly

on her failure to remember what she and Melanie talked about, it could so easily have turned out badly.'

'Ah, but you see, Robin, she had already made a far more damaging blunder than that, while she was telling me about her flat tyre. That was when she really tried to embroider and she wasn't cut out for it.'

'It sounded authentic enough to me, as you repeated it,' Toby said. 'I could picture the whole scene unrolling before my eyes.'

'Then you really can't have been on your toes, because one of the statements that unrolled was that she had wanted to telephone me to find a garage, but then she remembered that we'd moved to the Green Man. What was wrong about that?'

'Nothing. It was exactly what we had done.'

'Oh sure, but Viola couldn't have known that, could she? It was only decided on after she set out for London. So she must have come back and found our note, and it followed that her story was untrue from start to finish.'

'So all we need to ask now,' Robin said, 'is why did she do it?'

'Oh, can't you guess, Robin? Tessa was right all along. Elfrieda did not take the conventional route to heaven, Viola pushed her there.'

'Although once again it wasn't premeditated, it wasn't even murder. She had urgent business with Elfrieda that evening and she wanted to make sure they would not be disturbed. She's a pretty good mimic, as you know, and it was she who telephoned Mr Padmore's secretary and changed the appointment. Apart from that she'd done nothing underhand and she walked up the ramp quite openly, not much caring whether she were seen or not, since her mission, although not exactly friendly, was by no means hostile.'

'The mission being?'

'To have a straight talk with Elfrieda. She'd heard the rumours that Melanie was back in town and she guessed that it would only be a matter of time before Elfrieda relented and welcomed the prodigal home with open arms. Then all the quarrelling and discontent and Jamie's sulks would start up again and she wanted to nip it in the bud. She may not have been starry eyed about the Rotunda, but she certainly had a vested interest in seeing that it continued to flourish and she meant to do her utmost to make Elfrieda see reason. She probably expected her to be mildly shocked when there was a tap on the door and, instead of Mr Padmore, in sailed Viola, but unfortunately there had been a much more severe shock only minutes before and Elfrieda was still badly shaken up by it.'

'When, instead of Mr Padmore, in sailed Melanie?'

'Not only that, but unrecognisable at first, because of the man's wig and false moustache. She was fond of playing tricks like that and what I had failed to realise was that, in addition to being quite a competent actress, she was expert at disguise, able to fool even people who knew her well. And she threw herself into it with such enthusiasm that she used to borrow clothes and props from the wardrobe. However, to get back to Viola . . . . where was I?'

'She had just walked in instead of Mr Padmore.'

'Oh yes, and looking rather alarmingly stern and resolute, no doubt having keyed herself up for the interview. Anyway, it was all a little too much for the old lady, who promptly collapsed. I should guess that Viola was about ready to follow her, when she realised what an effect she'd had and it must have gone through her mind in a flash that if she were to go for help there would be all sorts of awkward questions to be answered as to what she was doing there, not to mention some even more unwelcome queries concerning Mr Padmore's telephone call. Just that kind of unpleasantness, in fact, which she had dedicated her life to avoiding. And, at a further guess, I'd say that it was then that Mr Padmore made his first attempt to ring the office, which he said he had tried to do for twenty minutes, and that this completely unnerved Viola. So she wheeled the chair on to the ramp, sent it on its way and then scuttled back to her dressing room. If the worst came to the worst and she met anyone on the way she could have explained that there'd been an accident and she was going for help. Otherwise, she'd bury herself in her book again and say nothing, which in fact is how it turned out.'

'And what was Melanie up to during all this?'

'She'd been sent into the back bedroom to remove her wig and make-up. That's not a guess, incidentally, it's the only plausible explanation for that false moustache on the dressing table.'

'And you think she popped her head round the door at the crucial moment?'

'Presumably. Which is also what makes me think it was then that Mr Padmore tried to ring up. I expect Melanie was starting to take off her disguise, feeling a bit deflated because her screamingly funny joke had fallen so flat and, when the phone went on ringing and Elfrieda didn't answer, she got really scared and opened the communicating door, probably just in time to see Viola going to work.'

'And then?'

'Realising that something sinister was afoot and that it would be to her disadvantage to be found on the premises, she climbed into the service lift, descended to ground floor level, let herself out by the emergency exit and then nipped off back to her little love nest in the grounds of Dene Cottage.'

'So that's where she holed up during her disappearing acts.'

'In that fisherman's hut, no less. It was empty, as you know. They found quite a few of her belongings there and I think she and Charlie had been using it on and off ever since she arrived in Dearehaven.'

'But what a fool she was to let on to Viola that she'd caught her in the act! She might have guessed that the reaction wouldn't be very cordial.'

'A guileless girl in many ways, but the terrifying part is that by doing so it was she who turned Viola into a murderess. Up till then, she'd been guilty of nothing worse than trying to avoid discord. She had a positive mania about life running smoothly for herself and everyone around her. That's why she feared and hated Melanie; almost prophetically, you might say, because in the end it was Melanie who forced her hand and landed her in the worst trouble of all.'

'So when she got murdered in her turn, you could say that she'd brought it on herself and only got her just deserts,' Robin suggested.

'Yes, I suppose you could.'

Toby looked rather depressed by this. Being so pessimistic, he does not like to hear of people's sins finding them out, still less of such examples of punishment fitting the crime. So, in an attempt to take his mind off these dismal subjects, I asked them:

'If this had been fiction, instead of merely truth, what would you have called it?'

'How about *Death in the Round*?' Robin suggested.

'Yes, that's not bad, because onions are round too, in a way, aren't they?'

'In a way, I suppose, but I'm not quite sure how they come into it.'

'Well, you see, Robin, the core of the whole matter was the character and personality of Melanie. Of Elfrieda, too, to some extent; she was a smaller onion. I never had a chance to get anywhere near the centres while they were alive, so I had to get other people to peel off one layer after another to find out what was underneath. And once I started, it really got a hold on me.'

'I'm no good at titles,' Toby said. 'I usually leave it to the girl who does my typing.'

'I wonder what she'd come up with for this one?'

'Oh, *The Onion Skin Murder*, I expect. She has the straightforward approach.'

'Well, that might do, I suppose. I'll have to think about it and give you my decision in the morning.'

'No hurry!' he said, brightening up as he saw the end in sight. 'Next week, any time at all will do just as well.'